KINGDOM
OF THE
GOLDEN TARA

Toby Smith

Cover illustrations by Toby Smith, Phillipe Velasquez,
and Masha Tatarintsev

ISBN: 148491676X
ISBN 13: 9781484916766

Dedicated to

those who nurture the Fairy spirit

Chapter One

"What are you doing?" the young, dark-haired man questioned.

At this moment in time, he preferred being nameless, especially in association with the young woman across the room. His longing for a more committed intimate relationship could not compete with her soul missions, and he did not wish to put more pressure on her. He watched her rummage through the room for her things like she was preparing for a long trip.

"Packing for Turkey," the young woman answered as she stuffed a few belongings in a travel pack. Slender in stature with light-brown hair, she shook her head at him, and feigned minor annoyance at his nosiness as she focused on her task. She wished that he would concern himself with ruling his own kingdom. Not about to surrender her independence in their casual, but steady friendship, she shunned any hint of commitment to anyone except her parents. For now she intended to remain an unknown, sensing that both history and the world would define them soon enough.

Unlike those around her, Nest moved into her potential as a world leader by instinct, zest, and passion. She had never chosen her destiny. Instead Nest just stepped into it, like a pair of shoes. Appreciating the work of her forebears in reseeding the kingdoms of Avalon and Camelon, she embraced their world in its six-hundred-year-old incarnation. The Serpentine Romans with their limited perspectives told the populace that they were in the years of 900 AD, but Nest's inherited legacy had a timeless quality. Only the proponents of the Roman Empire lived and died; whereas Nest and her tribes lived, partied, projected, travelled, ascended, endured, and wandered through various dimensions pertaining to time and the astral realm of their spiritual origins. They knew that they were from somewhere else, preferring to keep their distance on a chaotic planet. Lives and spirit had been lost to the conquering invaders. Lessons had been learned for survival. As long as they never engaged a Gray or Serpentine, mortality for Nest and her kingdom remained a relative term. They lived their lives simultaneously in the past, present, and future. Life wasn't about winning or losing; it was about being and existing. The requirements involved the ability to take the good with the bad, and continue progressing in the most productive manner. This required the lively art of isolating oneself from the Serpentines and their various forms of Gray. There was always the question of balance in this pursuit, which kept other alien manifestations or infestations in check. Nest's present mission was to restore equilibrium in a particular region of the world mired in serious decay.

"Without me?" he asked in mock annoyance before laughing and taking her in his arms.

She brightened in his embrace and looked into his eyes. "The abbot suggested taking Elissa."

The young man withdrew in lame protest. He told her, "That golden Sea Dragons gets to go everywhere with you."

"You have to stay here and lead your country," she reminded him. Sitting on the end of the bed in the room, the woman looked down at her things and threw a few more items in her bag. Her face grew serious.

"When do you leave?" he asked her as he sat down beside her.

"Tomorrow morning," she said. "I'm finishing up what my great-great-great grandmother started. Her name was Ingrod. Dad wants me to deal directly with a spiritual group there."

"Sounds like you are tying up loose ends, very old ones," the young man said as he sat down on the bed beside her.

Nest sighed, feeling the weight of the world on her shoulders. "Sea Dragons serve as record keepers, which is why I'm bringing Elissa. The abbot asked me to jog her memory as well. Much information has been lost over the past thousand years. They want me to shift through the debris of meaningless myth, legend, religion, and alternate history. The elders gave me the task of determining what is true, so we know what is important enough to move forward in time. The Kingdom of the Golden Tara needs a firm foundation for its protection. Like my great-aunt Creirwy, I have become the designated archivist for the Dragon Flyer technology, which probably originated long before Ingrod's father, King Cole, built Camelon after the Romans attacked his grandmother Boudacia near

Camelodium. I would not be surprised to learn that the Dragon Flyer technology goes as far back in time as Gondwanaland."

"I suppose that there is something to be said for writing one's memoirs," her companion mused.

"Not really," she asserted, rising from the bed. "Memoirs are usually written to hide information. My elders have convinced me that the past is the key to the future. My mission pertains to finding that past. The Druid version of history is so intertwined with the views scribed by the Roman legal entities that I must unscramble the relationships in order to successfully sever our ties. They write the myths, religions, and legends, while we tell our history through stories. I want a clear break with the people who murdered my ancestors. Cuscraid, one of Creirwy's lovers, insisted that we separate ourselves. I agree with his vision. Cuscraid, as you may recall, is the grandson of the mutant merman that the Roman legal entities crucified."

"I do remember," he quietly confessed. "That tragedy left an indelible mark on the spirit of the planet. However, it successfully reseeded light into human existence. I'm not sure how, but it is there."

After pausing for a moment to reflect, he suggested, "Let's take a walk in the moonlight. You look like you could use a distraction like me. Sea Dragons can't keep you as warm at night as I can."

She smiled and turned toward the young man. Putting her things aside, she leaned closer to him and kissed him deeply. Then she stood before the man and offered her hand. "Let's go!"

He grinned widely and accepted her hand. Hurrying to his feet, he stood beside the woman and twirled her lightly around the room. Then he put an arm around her and ushered her out the door. They giggled and raced through the abbey corridor for the courtyard. When they were outside in the moonlight, they danced a little under the starry sky. Arm in arm they walked toward the meadow with a skip in their steps.

Suddenly, they noticed several people run past them for the crowd gathering in the opposite direction.

"There's a party on the Hill of Tara," the young man observed, wishing to keep his interaction with the woman on the light side. Any function on the Hill of Tara implied important business. By this time in world history, nobody could recall whether tara meant 'tear' or 'terrain'. Nest reasoned that it was because it no longer mattered. The terms had fused into an entirely new concept where passages in life were defined by the shedding of healthy tears. The Hill of

Tara marked the site where the leaders of Atlantean refugees had adopted the surviving human family as their own relations. The high kings and queens of Ireland, who descended from chiefs of the Atlantean exodus, intermarried with the remaining Hebrew tribe of Dan.

Nest's great-aunt Crierwy and grandmother Tinka had established the timeless Kingdom of the Golden Tara from the ashes of Camelon and Avalon. As descendants of King Arthur, both recognized that dreams were sometimes manifested through blood, sweat, and tears. The women left this spiritual construct as a multidimensional temple for their kingdom. Their path led to ecstasy, or the presence of heaven on earth. They knew that the Serpentine Romans would never find them there.

"Ready?" the woman asked, knowing that she was obligated to attend.

"Let's go!" he encouraged her. "Tonight is the night."

"Every night is a special one at the Hill of Tara," she mused. Deciding to make the most of the looming situation, she said, "Look, they have already started dancing. This beats packing."

"Don't worry. I can help you tomorrow morning," he offered.

The woman blushed lightly with her companion's innuendo. She replied, "It's a deal."

They quickly walked toward the gathering. The crowd appeared thickest around Lia Fail, a large stone pillar also called the Stone of Destiny. People were touching it and whispering in awe.

"Lia Fail has been continuously humming," the couple overheard someone say.

The young woman dropped her companion's hand and headed for her father, who was closely examining the pillar. The stone glowed softly as she approached. Noticing the stone's response to the newcomer, people stepped away. A soft whistle emanated from the stone.

The young woman heard the whistle and froze. Then she turned and ran back down the hill. An emerging crowd blocked her escape. This time the stone whistled a loud catcall. The young woman's mother appeared from the group and hugged her closely.

"We suspected that the Stone of Destiny might skip a generation," her mother explained. "Time to turn and face the music."

The young woman ignored her. Straightening in her mother's embrace, she demanded, "I want to talk to the golden Sea Dragon queen. I was just beginning to have fun."

"Did someone ask for me?" Elissa, the Sea Dragon queen, asked as she slowly approached the young woman. "I had a feeling that tonight was going to be good night."

Turning her back to the Stone of Destiny, the young woman left her mother and faced Elissa. "There's more to this trip to Turkey than I know, isn't there?"

"Yes," Elissa agreed nonchalantly with a toss of her golden-scaled head. "You'll need to visit the Rhakotis Library first to catch up on some reading. Maybe a few history lessons as well. Now, go touch the Stone of Destiny and see if it hums three times before you set off the party."

The young woman did as Elissa instructed. The Stone of Destiny glowed under her touch and responded with three distinct hums. The young woman immediately drew back, took a deep breath, and faced the crowd, which was getting larger by the minute.

"We have a new queen. It's Nest ferch Cadell!" voices in the crowd shouted. Others echoed, "Finally, we have found Creirwy's successor!"

The young man, Elise, went to Nest and tossed her in his arms. He lightly danced with her across the top of the hill. Delighted by the sight of her companion, Nest quickly forgot the crowd, which had immediately dispersed to rouse the rest of the inhabitants for further carousing. Soon the entire countryside was filled with late night festivities.

"About time," everyone whispered to each other in the darkness. Overjoyed by the divine mandate to move on, people danced the night away. Nest and her lover left the party a few hours before dawn. Meanwhile, the festivities escalated.

Nest's father, King Cadell, gazed at the young couple in the distance as they walked away. They were returning to Nest's private room. Cadell's life partner, Patty, who had prevented the young queen from fleeing down the hill, stood by his side. He put his arm around the mother's shoulder and directed her attention to their departing daughter.

Patty said, "I saw it coming when she was born, nine months after our night at Eamhain Mhacha."

The ancient Celtics had constructed Eamhain Mhacha for astral projection and other spiritual purposes. Years ago, Nest's great-aunt, Queen Creirwy, had popularized the sacred mound with her lover, Cuscraid, who served as priest as well as an Irish chieftain. Now it had become a favorite destination for honeymoons and wedding anniversaries. Queen Crierwy of Wales, the daughter of King David, or Dewi, doubled as a nun and abbess. Until his untimely assassination, King Dewi, the grandson of King Arthur, had led many lives.

Not only did he roam the streets of Wales as a bard, he was both a monk and soldier. He continued the Dragon Flyer tradition of being a spiritual warrior, which Crierwy had assumed. Although the Serpentines, or remnants of Constantine's Holy Roman Empire managed the religious orders, the local Celtic and Druid natives successfully hid their offspring in various monasteries and nunneries, where they continued to nurture their spirituality. In this manner they maintained a relationship with their soul origins in the galaxies, which the Serpentine Romans preferred writing out of their history books. Unlike the natives, the Serpentines had a lot to hide from the populace, which continued to grow more and more ignorant of their own varied intergalactic heritage.

Cadell glanced down and softly kissed her head with a gentle hug. Though he had always suspected that Nest had been conceived at Eamhain Mhacha, he never had heard it mentioned until now. He chuckled lightly, "Yes, Mom always said that Crierwy had found a fresh start there. Now I think we all have a new beginning."

"Grandma Tinka said that?" Patty laughed. "We all miss her and Crierwy, even though they have ascended. It has been twenty years. Nest arrived in the world shortly before they both boarded the spaceship."

"Oh, that reminds me," Caudal said. "Creirwy wanted me to give her ruby ring to her successor. She must have sensed that it would be Nest."

"We did our work," Patty remarked.

"Ah, Patty, we did a great job," he told his life partner with a kiss. Then he pointed to a lone figure in the distant shadows. "Merfyn seems to be the only one who isn't dancing."

"I know." Patty sighed. "We must keep watch on that one—the great-grandson of Tristan. He serves as Esyllt's courier. She claims to been held captive by the exiled King of Cornwall, but those who know King Mark say otherwise. In England they call her Morgasia. They say that she is very much like her sister, Morgan Le Fey. They were the nieces of the traitor, Hen Coel, the King of Colchester. He is known to the Roman Britons as King Coleus. Her cousin, Helena, King Coleus's daughter, partnered with Constantius and their son became the Emperor Constantine."

"He has been congenial with those at the Hill of Tara, though I think that he has his ambitions focused on Ceridig's kingdom," Cadell commented. "Hen Coel's other daughter married Cunneda, Ceridig's father. I suspect that Esyllt would like to place her adopted son and courier there."

"It was Ceridig's soldiers that killed King Dewi, the son of King Arthur's and Creirwy's father," Patty reminded him. "Creirwy barely escaped Ceridig's kingdom herself."

Without a further word, King Cadell motioned for one of the guards to track Merfyn. He quietly said to Patty, "Remember, the Celtics are survivors from Atlantis, who narrowly escaped the diabolical experiments of the Serpentines and the dark forces in the galaxies. We all have a huge task, keeping our new Queen of the Universe safe and protected."

Chapter Two

After flying under cloud cover to a series of portals that led to Egypt, Nest entered the Rhakotis Library. She peered through the corridors and rows of book stacks. The place was empty and her footsteps echoed eerily down the halls.

"It is difficult to imagine that this old library once bustled with the affairs of Prince Gerwyn at the tender age of three," Nest recalled. "It seems too sterile for a roving youngster. I can't picture Queen Joslin chasing a toddler here while on her honeymoon. Obviously, the couple found inspiration here, otherwise they never would have got around to having my Grandmother Tinka, Gerwyn's younger sister."

"I was there," Elissa quipped. "So was Alfie."

"Do you mean Alfred the Great?" Nest inquired.

"Yes, he was babysitting Gerwyn at the time."

Nest shook her head in amazement then she focused on her immediate mission. "So, why I am here at the Rhakotis Library?" she asked Elissa. "Why is it so important to come here before going to Turkey?"

"Well, we want to break in our queens gently," Elissa explained. "You need some background information on the Mu'tazili."

The Sea Dragon queen scurried to a long hallway where someone had painted the significant history of the planet earth. Following closely behind Elissa, Nest breezed past the drawings until they arrived at a scene of a cave in present day Saudi Arabia. There were three men in the cave conducting an intense meeting.

"Who are these people?" she asked.

"One is Alli, a mutant merman, one is an orphaned Arab, and another is an Anglo," replied Elissa.

"Looks like the Anglo still has his Celestial glow," Nest commented, outlining the features of the man with her index finger.

"Yes, the Arab mistook him for the light being, known as Gabriel," Elissa noted. "He was a member of Ingrod's family in Germany. Ingrod, King Arthur's grandmother, was a second generation Celestial from the Angles region. A linguistic error caused their Roman enemies to confuse the word 'Angles' with 'angel'. Due to the purity of their spiritual nature, the Angles did resemble their Celestial forebears, so it was an easy mistake for the panicked Roman soldiers, who held a de-evolutionary bias. After Ingrod died, the Anglo in the picture took her place as an emissary."

"Was Alli related to Jesse, the point person for the spiritual evolution of the human family?" Nest inquired. "The Roman Serpentines crucified the mutant merman to stifle an insurrection in Jerusalem. He had been adopted and raised by the Jewish royal family."

"Alli was a cousin. Both were mutant mermen. Their mission was to heal the planet by bringing light to the world, but they were like fish out of water. Three hundred years after the fiasco in Jerusalem, they tried it again in Turkey. Ingrod helped place Alli among a human family there. This time, the mutant merman was placed with descendants of Moses, who were from Dinah's tribe. They called him Nikolaos, in honor of his mentor Uncle Nikolaos, a bishop in the area. Ingrod enjoyed calling him Santa Claus after her father, ol' King Cole. King Cole's nickname was Claus, an endearing term used by his German wife. You can certainly see the Northern European influence in Alli's attire. Ingrod taught him how to be a Dragon flyer, though Alli preferred reindeer after his visit to Norway. His cousin, the famous wizard Merilyn, was living in Norway at the time."

"What happened at the meeting?" she asked the Sea Dragon queen.

"Alli tried to persuade the Arab to drop his sociopolitical movement for purposes of spiritual evolution," Elissa continued.

"Did it work? Was he able to convince the Arab?" Nest questioned.

"Only partially," Elissa answered. "The mixed result was 'Slam.'"

"Oh, they slammed it all right." Nest sighed, taking a deep breath. "I will have to speak to them about this. The Arab world is turning on the human family."

"I know. We must clue them in," Elissa agreed. "They are chasing their own tail, or maybe I should say, their own *tale*. They are part of our human family."

"Somebody has got to set them straight," Nest announced.

"You're looking at 'em. See the face in the mirror of my body armor," Elissa stated. "It is our next mission to explain the situation to them."

Noticing her reflection in Elissa's shiny scales, Nest rose from her kneeling position before the drawings. She looked at Elissa dead in the eye and asked, "Us?"

"Yes. Any more history lessons?" Elissa politely asked her. "Especially now that you understand the significance of your mission to Patara, Turkey. There is an old Dragon flyer base there from the days of the intergalactic wars of ancient Egypt. Those wars wrought such devastation on the planet that water from the oceans splashed into the atmosphere. Rings of ice encircled the globe, like those on Saturn. The earth spirits of other dimensions refer to the intergalactic wars of ancient Egypt as the Lord of the Rings. Someday, a man named Tolkein will retrieve this memory from his DNA and write a book about it. Unless it has been altered irretrievably, the past is part of our identity. I think that you will enjoy Yuletide festivities in Patara. Just think of it as another party."

"So, I am traveling from the Hill of Tara to Patara," Nest surmised as she examined more drawings. "That sounds like a gridding opportunity to me. The ancient spiritual art of gridding involves the creation of lines of energy that connect various spots on the planet. Depending on who does the gridding, the result is either evolutionary or a catastrophic. Serpentines grid for spiritual annihilation, which we consider a catastrophe. We, as result of our innate identity, can do no other except to grid for purposes of spiritual evolution. Camelon represented the last bastion of gender balance on the planet, which went dormant like Avalon, its feminine counterpart."

"Yes, you are tying up loose ends. Patara is code for *father's tears*," said Elissa. "You are to give the golden tara to a young priest in Patara. He is destined to be the first Pope Nicholas. The town is vacant now, except for Nicholas and his Elves. The inhabitants fled the Byzantines. Meanwhile, Nicholas seized the opportunity to set up shop and launch his papal career."

"Nikolaos is Greek for gift-bearer," Nest realized. "I'd like to bring this young priest with me to Arabia. Apparently part of the mission pertains to the restoration of gender balance. It needs to be reseeded in the area."

"Don't forget Alli, Jesse's cousin, the mutant merman that the Arabs confuse with an angel," Elissa piped. "He comes in handy when meeting with Arabs or Persians."

They left the Rhakotis Library and journeyed to Patara. Nest flew on the back of Elissa, who knew the route well and used several portals for short cuts.

When they landed in Patara, Elissa pointed Nest in the direction of the town church and left to forage in the abandoned town. Nest slowly made her way to a door on the side of the building.

"There you are!" a young man in black robes greeted. "I saw the golden Sea Dragon queen in the sky and knew that you were coming."

Delightedly, he led her inside the sacristy where it was warm. Offering the young woman a chair, he provided food and drink as he sat down across the small table. The sacristy was heavily decorated with boughs of evergreens and gold tinsel.

Nest looked around the room briefly before she began. Removing the golden tara from her cloak, she placed it on the table. She told the young priest, "This is for you. I understand that you have an interesting career ahead of you."

The man accepted the golden tara. Holding it in his hands, Nicholas grimaced as he closely examined it. "I am going to need this. We are beginning the dark ages here. What is the immortal goddess Kuan Yin up to these days?"

"Busy setting up the next leg of our journey," Nest replied. "You get to come with me. Ever flown on a Sea Dragon before?"

"No, but I always dreamed that I would someday," Nicholas replied. "Alli hasn't got that far in our classes. There are so many other things to learn for the papacy."

"Wonderful!" Nest said enthusiastically. "I will be your teacher."

"First, I need a history lesson," he protested. "Tell me more about the significance of the golden tara. I understand that you are gridding Patara."

"Initially, the icon soothed a mother's tears," Nest explained. "Kuan Yin gave it to Queen Joslin after she had been up all night with a fussy newborn. That infant was my grandmother Tinka, who later became Queen Twyanwedd or Tudlwystl, depending on whether you are in Wales, Scotland, Ireland, or England."

Pausing a moment, Nest took a deep breath and stared briefly at the masculine decor of the room. "When Camelon fell, the spiritual community center was moved from Avebury to Stonehenge. This spiritual base networked with other sacred sites around the globe like Easter Island and Machu Picchu. Now we are tying up loose ends with the Avebury network and going for the big picture, which is the manifestation of Camelon's promise in the next generation. Both Tinka and Crierwy worked to grid the Soul Transport Network with the Kingdom of the Golden Tara. The task of carrying on their work is my destiny. I am promoting gender balance in the Kingdom of the Golden Tara."

Nest glanced down at the ruby ring on the young priest's finger. He noticed her gaze and admitted, "I have already been recruited. Nikolaos told me a few details, but I wanted to hear it from your lips. Our rings match." Then the man rose from his chair and carefully packed the icon away in his travel pack. Without a word, he offered his hand to Nest and escorted her out of the building. They found Elissa munching on some evergreen boughs that decorated the town square. Most of the people had fled the area due to the recent Arab raids. Those that had remained were part of Alli's Dragon flyer team.

"There's jolly ol' Nikolaos," the young priest greeted as he embraced the man who was feeding Elissa the evergreen boughs. "Feeding the poor."

"Don't worry, Lucky," the large white-bearded man chuckled to the aspiring pope. "The Elves will be happy to replace them." Then he turned toward Nest and extended a hearty hug. "You can call me Alli. Let's go restore balance to Basrah. They will rename it Al-Basrah when we are done."

"Lucky?" Nest confronted the young man. "You never told me that your name was Lucky."

The aspiring pope shrugged with a grin. "I was born lucky, and survived a Serpentine attack on my village as a small infant. Everyone else was killed. After giving me a three leaf clover, Patrick baptized me and eventually set me up in the monastery here."

Nest cocked her head at Elissa, who refused to elaborate. Nest remarked, "That's attitude for you. Rather than focus on the tragedy, you accepted the nickname 'Lucky'." Deciding to change the subject, she asked, "Do you think I will need a veil? I only wear one when a disguise is appropriate."

"No, let them see your dark red hair and light skin. They will think that you are Gabriel," Alli suggested.

"Don't forget to wield the sword that Creirwy left you," Elissa added. "We must cut some dead weight in Persia."

Nest nervously glanced at the group. Elissa's admission caught her off guard. She wondered about what she would find in Basrah—the place where the first human forms were fashioned from clay.

"Don't look at me. I'm not brandishing a sword," Lucky protested. "I'm a man of the cloth."

"I'm a woman of the cloth, but it is only another alias," Nest said, figuring out her strategy. "I can see that I play the role of guardian here."

"Nothing like the angel of divine justice brandishing a fiery sword to make a point," Nikolaos summarized. Then he hollered, "Oh, Rudolph! Time to go to Persia."

Chapter Three

"Don't you just love synchronicity?" Lucky asked Nest as she strapped him on Elissa's back. "Everything fits together, and events line up perfectly in the universe. We even have matching rings and matching missions."

"The meaningful play of events tells us that we are on track," she agreed. "Though sometimes the results overwhelm me with the starkness of the truth. Obviously we were meant to find each other, though I never dreamed that I would travel to Persia with flying reindeer."

"Not to mention a golden dragon," Lucky added, reminding her of his perspective.

The golden Sea Dragon queen extended her great wings and lifted her flyers to the heights above. Alli flew on Rudolph's back. He smiled and waved at them as the flying reindeer lit the skies with his red nose.

"Don't mind Rudolph," Alli grinned. "He's special."

Nest nodded at him. The animals that helped often were born with special features that would eventually become a blessing for the generations they served. This evolution provided an ongoing tactical advantage, because it was adaptive to changing conditions.

When they landed in Persia, the trio went to the site that many knew as the Garden of Eden. However, it wasn't really much of a garden. When the first human prototype was created, it was a bog of mud and clay. Eventually, the river retreated and vegetation grew, but it wasn't as lush as other places on the planet. The site had been chosen for the convenience of the artist.

"This where the trouble first began," Nest commented as she strolled the grounds. She thought for a moment before deciding, "With hindsight being perfect vision, a few corrections are compelling."

Lucky jumped to the next conclusion. "The human form was created by a Pleiadian. The Pleiadians also provided the Ring of Power during one of the seven days of creation, but there was one more gift they bestowed on the Earth's inhabitants. These rings represented spiritual gifts and were destroyed after the virtue became embodied in human form. Later, the dark forces made rings for mind-control, which were used during the intergalactic wars of ancient Egypt. It was the time of the Lord of the Rings, which also pertained to the existence of several ice rings around the planet. As above, so below. For several thousand years, Earth looked like Saturn."

"What do you mean?" Nest asked.

Alli left the partners for his own tour while they conferred. Being the closest human form to a light being, he was not responsible for its evolution. He came only to serve and promote the natural health of the planet.

"It has to do with the Draco Constellation, the place where the Celestial refugees met to create the planet," Lucky explained. "The apple tree of the Genesis myth existed originally in the constellation, except the fruit wasn't really an apple. The golden spheres guarded by the great stellar dragon contained *knowledge*, which was in important in the desperate race for technology. Several myths, like the one in Genesis, bring Heaven to Earth in this area. Knowing that the human form had been made under duress, the Pleiadians gave the planet a Sacred Tree."

"Another gift-bearer," Nest remarked, noting the present theme of this gridding system. "Where is this Sacred Tree?"

"In Australia," Lucky replied. "The Aboriginals guard it."

"Why do they call it the Sacred Tree?" she asked.

"Medicine made from the tree severs the chains that have evolved around human consciousness," he told her. "They call it the Boab Tree."

"Why is it in Australia?" she questioned. "They could use it here to break some of the negativity that is being passed through generations."

"I know," he agreed. "The Pleiadians thought that it would be safer if it was remotely located until the time was ripe."

"I must go there soon," Nest realized with a nod.

Elissa agreed. "Now I think humans would appreciate the gift of the Sacred Tree. You can incorporate it in the gridding system that Queen Joslin started."

Lucky smiled in delight. His steps lightened as he walked through the site. "Progress," he happily rejoined. "Please, do it before I get elected pope."

Kneeling on the ground to study the mud, Nest turned and eyed him wryly. She remained passionate about her present mission. "Oh, don't worry. I'm sure I'll do more than that. Now, where is that group of Mu'tazili?"

"They are waiting for us in the city," Elissa offered. "We'll have to walk to the temple. The streets here are very narrow."

They met the Mu'tazili at the local mosque. The mosque consisted of a large circular room with a domed top. A group of bearded men resembling rabbis surrounded her as they entered the large room.

"Why are you meeting us here?" Nest asked, getting straight to the point. "You are Jewish."

"I know," one bearded man replied, "but, we'll go down in the history as 'Slams.'"

"What do you mean?" Nest questioned. Then she asked rhetorically, "Are you the only rational ones left?"

"Yes, they call us *Rationalists*," the spokesperson answered for the group. "We are trying to reform the movement."

"What is this about the local leader killing a new wife every night?" Nest asked.

"He's quite famous, you know," the bearded man told her. "They are writing a book about him. He has been at it for over a thousand nights. I think they are calling the book, *Nights of Arabia*."

"Have you lost your minds?" she questioned further. "Your civilization was once so spiritually endowed that you traversed the globe on flying carpets. What happened?"

Becoming impatient, Nest left the group and paced to the other end of the mosque. Elissa tried to calm her down. The group of bearded men whispered among themselves, eventually staring off quietly into space.

"Look at your implant," Elissa instructed, pointing to the pulsating dark object underneath Nest's flesh.

Nest calmed down and examined her upper left thigh. Exposing the skin to the ambient light of the room, Nest watched the buried object track the dome above her. Her free arm drifted toward it as if there was a magnetic attraction. Though she could alter the pain threshold with her mind, the flesh around the embedded object ached until her entire body was in alignment with the dome. She noticed the group of male Mu'tazili grow faint from watching her movements. Within seconds, they had all passed out.

Lucky grinned, "They can't handle Gabriel's naked flesh."

"They don't know what they are missing," Alli chuckled. "They should bring angels to the church more often."

Feeling self-conscious, Nest immediately dropped the hem of her cloak. She addressed the rest of her entourage. "Lucky, did you know that you had an implant next to your heart? I can detect the vibration from your chest. By the way Alli, where did you get that object pulsating out of the skin of your cheek?"

Suddenly, the men quit laughing. They somberly timed the beating implants under their skin and walked around. The amplitude of the pulse was a harmonic with their distance from the ceiling. Noting the direction that the dark object tracked, both simultaneously pointed to the dome of the mosque.

After retrieving the sword from her travel pack, Nest quickly sliced her thigh and removed the tiny object from her skin. A tear fell from Elissa's face. It rolled down her snout and landed on the open wound, sealing it shut. Nest displayed the object in the palm of her hand. The object danced a few centimeters in the air toward the dome. Nest instantly closed her palm to prevent the object from flying away. "It's a piece of the rock!" she cried.

Chapter Four

"One less implant," Nest remarked as she lowered the object to the floor and wielded her sword.

The sword struck the object in midair, slicing though the center of the stone. The Y-shaped object turned as red as Rudolph's glowing nose. After a few seconds, the implant shattered in a minor explosion before it hit the earth.

"Dad was right," she observed. "He told me that Crierwy's sword could cut through anything. I heard that she even used it to highlight some of the Nazca lines. The sword worked well for the finer details."

"The implant has the same composition as the meteorite in the dome, or at least what the locals have been calling a meteor," Lucky noted, gazing at the roof over his head. He had been present during the construction of several mosques and churches in Turkey. He knew that each one contained a rock fragment from a larger rocky dome in Jerusalem.

"Lemuria, the site of present day Madagascar, was not sunk by a meteor. This fragment is not a meteorite," she reminded him. "The Serpentines sunk the island with their lasers. Both the dome and the implant contain a piece of molten bedrock from after the time the Serpentines struck Lemuria with their lasers. It's an insult. Not only did the Serpentines plant this hideous reminder of the attack in the skin of every human being, but they had humans insert it in every place of worship."

"The Serpentines used the same laser weapons when they razed the Second Temple of Jerusalem," Alli recalled. "They created a place of worship from the molten rock. Go figure."

"I think the locals have more implants than the average earthling," Nest observed. "Their souls must have suffered much more extensive trauma during transport. I only have two left, but I can count at least seven *visible* implants on the bodies of the unconscious Mu'tazili. Look at how their skin pulsates under the dome!"

"May I borrow your sword?" Lucky asked, changing the subject. "I want to cut mine from my heart."

Nest took a deep breath, shooting Elissa a questioning glance by raising her eyebrows and nodding. She wasn't sure about lending her sword for a risky purpose. Even if the man was Lucky, Nest did not want any more blood on her sword. Elissa ignored her pleading glance. Instead the golden Sea Dragon queen deferred to Nikolaos.

"Here, let me help you with that," Nikolaos offered. "I can use the implant in my cheek to magnetize the one near Lucky's heart. Nest can make the cut and I will help with the extraction." Approaching the golden Sea Dragon queen, he implored, "Elissa, can you spare a few more tears. I want mine out, too."

"Once they have been activated, the implants are easier to remove and destroy," Nest commented as she sliced Lucky's chest.

Blood oozed from the tissue around the exposed Y-shaped object embedded in the tissue. Nikolaos leaned over Lucky's chest and the implant began to pull away from the tissue. Nest caught the moving implant in the air with the tip of her sword. The young woman whacked the implant with her blade and destroyed it. Cutting Nikolaos's cheek open, she tore out his implant. Her sword caught the implant in the air as Elissa shed tears over the wounds.

By the time, the last implant had been destroyed, the group of Mutazili regained consciousness. Several of the men watched the explosion and fainted again. Nest walked over to the group recovering on the floor of the mosque. She stood over the spokesperson, who had missed the last exploding implant.

"Time to wake up. Take me to your leader," she demanded. Turning to Elissa and the others, she commented, "I want to get this over with. Tonight will be the thousandth and first night."

"Sure thing, Gabriel," the spokesperson answered, jumping to his feet. "The caliph will be really happy to see Allah, the hero of our worship."

"It isn't what you think. I'm not an angel," Nest argued, crossing her arms.

Refusing to quibble over details, the group of Mu'tazili ignored her protest. This was the most excitement that they had experienced their entire lives. They quickly roused the others and helped them to their feet.

Overhearing his words, Alli winked at Nest as they hurried out of the mosque. He told the young woman, "They only see what they *want* to see."

"Sometimes," she retorted. "You win this round. You can have them. The problem arises in separating out Dinah's tribe from Lilith's followers. Lilith made a deal with the devil, you know. She traded her soul to the Serpentines for a bite of knowledge when she was not ready for the information. We call them reality bites, and a human can have too much. It is important to live within your limits. We would have broken it to them soon enough, gradually, so that it wasn't such a shock for those mud-made creatures. Afterwards, Lilith could really see the difference between good and evil, which shocked her system. The Serpentines gained the ability to access her dream-state. She overdosed on negativity, and gave away valuable information to the Serpentines. Plus, she became an asset for their agenda. There *is* free choice, and that was embodied in the Boab Tree of Freedom. Love makes a choice, rather than seeks domination. Domination is the Serpentine agenda, which is why we left them to create our own planet. We don't want to play by those rules. It is not fun when your planet is destroyed because someone wants to control and manipulate you. Why bother existing at that point? This is why the Tree of Life was put next to the Tree of Knowledge. It was Plan B, in case the templates failed the test run."

"Let me intercede," Lucky said. "We'll see who swims and who drowns."

Elissa sauntered behind them in the streets. Shopkeepers tossed her helpings of food as she followed them. They wanted to be sure that the large Sea Dragon remained well fed. Hearing the commotion in the street, the caliph rushed outside of his grand tent to meet Nest at the entrance.

"This is your last night," Nest told him. "End of story. No more wives for you. Either move on or talk to Alli."

"I'll talk to Alli," the caliph confessed.

Alli stepped forward. "Look caliph, this isn't a sociopolitical movement. We are looking for a spiritual revolution, especially within the original human family. You can help Sindbad find the Boab Tree."

"That should do it," Lucky remarked. "Wait, who is Sindbad?"

"A sailor I met a few days ago. He was moaning on the docks," Alli said. "He is not a happy camper. I told him how to turn this sociopolitical situation around."

"I know Sindbad," the spokesperson for the Mu'tazili said. "He is reasonable."

"The spokesperson for the Mu'tazili is in charge now," Alli announced. Then he turned to the spokesperson, "Make sure that he marries no more women."

"I'll have him sail with Sindbad tomorrow," the spokesperson said. "Sindbad is sailing the Seven Seas. That should change the story of the Arabian Nights."

"At the very least," Lucky interjected.

"Nothing like the Seven Seas to help a man forget his problems," Alli, the mutant merman, continued. "Tell Sindbad that I'll put in a good word for him with the fish. I'm great with sailors."

"Thanks be to Almighty!" the caliph shouted. "A new story is a new life."

"Let's get out of here before I throw up," Nest decided. "I am ready to find that Boab Tree. The women here could use a dose. I don't know why they put up with this stuff."

"Many are descendants of Lilith," Lucky explained. "They willingly adopted the Serpentine agenda."

"No small wonder," Nest remarked. "Looks like they are still paying the price through mutual dissatisfaction. That's what happens when you fill your head with rocks."

"We'll turn Sindbad into a new man," Alli said. "He's the real prophet in training. I'll make sure that he profits." He chuckled at his play on words.

"Sounds like a great idea," Nest agreed. "He can remind Arabia of its original grandeur through his stories and adventures. We'll see if the caliph holds his own. End of story."

"I think *his* real name is Sindbad also," the spokesperson revealed.

"But, only one returns," Alli announced. He asked the spokesman pointedly, "Now, what is your name?"

The spokesperson puffed his chest in the air and decided, "Sindbad."

"That's the idea." Alli congratulated him.

"I thought that the sailor's name was Muhamid," a member of the group whispered to another man. A minor discussion ensued among the members.

"It's Sindband," the new Sindbad insisted. "It makes it easier for the transition of property and authority."

"Let's do it," the group agreed as they rubbed elbows with each other.

"I'm leaving," Nest decided. She turned toward Lucky, "Want a ride back to Turkey?"

"Sure thing," the young priest answered as he mounted Elissa.

"You can finish setting up Sindbad of the Seven Seas," Nest told Alli. "Have fun."

"Gabriel!" the Mu'tazili shouted. "Where are you going? Don't you want to stay for the celebration?"

"No, thanks," Nest replied as she strapped Lucky to the back of Elissa. "I'm going to do some research on the Boab Tree."

"Come visit me when I'm Pope Nicholas." Lucky waved to the Mu'tazili. "I'll need your assistance on a few matters. I can show you around the papacy."

"It's a deal!" they yelled in unison.

Chapter Five

Nest dropped Lucky off at the steps of the church. She untied the straps holding him to Elissa and helped him from the back of the Sea Dragon. Jumping down to the ground, he landed on his feet and planted himself firmly on the icy street. A sudden flurry of snowflakes fell from the sky, enveloping them in a thick white swirl. The snow fell faster and faster, accentuating their isolation in the empty town. Lucky stared into Nest's eyes for a brief moment. The abrupt change in weather frightened her because it grimly reminded her of the lonely coldness that she must confront in the world. Recognizing the look of hysterical fear, he placed a soft kiss on her cheek and hugged her. Her head fell against his chest as she sighed deeply.

"Where do we go from here?" she asked. "I am scared that I won't have the strength that I need to face the despair and overcome it."

Holding her in his arms, he looked up at the snow that pelted the ground. He could not see past her figure. He assured her, "I feel the same."

"Hold me," Nest said. "I don't want to leave you."

"Go find the Boab Tree," he answered. "I want to come with you."

She looked up at him, "You do? I don't have a clue where to begin looking for it."

"I've seen enough in the past few days," he said. "I'm convinced that we all need our freedom."

"Great," she said, putting her arms around his neck. However, the closer she came to him, the further away he seemed. She puzzled over emerging her role in this inevitable partnership. Though he had been born in the neighboring town of Myra, Nicholas had been adopted by surviving Druid tribes, who placed their offspring in Celtic monasteries. Celtic priests like Nicholas never swore to

25

celibacy in the Serpentine tradition, even if they aspired to be pope. They defied the rules of those who had violated their country. Elise, Nest's childhood friend at the Hill of Tara had always been more interested in her than she had been in him. Destiny called her away from the young man who hung around her as if he was her self-designated significant other. Like a new pair of shoes, Nest realized that part of her journey implied that she examine this partnership for its depth and perspective. She added, "I noticed that you and I had similar rings."

"That's right, sister," he replied, tightening his arms around her.

"We must talk about this some time," she said languidly.

"Let's get out of the cold," he told her. "I know where to start."

"Great," Nest repeated. She admitted ruefully, "This role came to me unexpectedly. The Stone of Destiny skipped a generation."

"I pursued it and it came to me, like a gift," he acknowledged. "Like the wonderful arrival of you and your Sea Dragon. It is like Christmas."

"Ahem," Elissa interrupted. "You might try looking in Australia."

"Oh yes, Australia," Lucky remembered. "Can you take us straight to the Boab Tree?"

"Yes. Climb aboard," the golden Sea Dragon queen offered.

"Why didn't you say so?" Nest asked.

"I wanted to see you two get better reacquainted," she replied as Nest reattached Lucky to her back.

Nest didn't respond. She wasn't sure what to make of the situation. The snow continued to fall heavily. Glancing at the empty stone church, she realized how cold the town had become. She shuddered slightly at the thought of looking for any warmth within such a structure. Convinced that there was nowhere left to go, she sighed. "I'll have to trust you on this one," she whispered in Elissa's ear.

"Trust me. It's the next lesson in your training," she softly said, so that Lucky would not overhear her.

Nest replied, "I thought that I was done. We'll have to discuss this later, when we are not in the middle of a blizzard."

Elissa's eyes sparkled and she nodded. She told Nest, "You are not the first Dragon flyer that felt that way. It seems to run in your family."

Nest ignored her and carefully climbed on her back. Nothing seemed to matter except the need to get out of the cold. After Nest settled behind Lucky, Elissa lifted her great golden wings and soared high into the dark blue sky above the snow-filled clouds.

They landed in a portion of Australia that had been known as Gondwanaland sixty-five million years ago. Lucky and Nest dismounted and stared at the rugged terrain. A large, solitary tree with a swollen truck stood several yards away.

"It resembles a large bottle," Nest said in awe. She walked around the tree cautiously to examine it.

"It is known as the Sacred Tree," Elissa remarked. "Here, try a leaf."

Nest removed a leaf from a branch and handed it to Lucky. Then she gently cut one from the tree for herself. Lifting the palmate leaf to her nose, she whiffed its fragrance. "It's a little different," she said as she rubbed her fingers on the soft underside of the leaf. "Here, let's solarize it in some water for several hours while we check out the local swimming hole."

Without waiting for the others, Nest began walking toward the gorge with the small waterfall. Raising the leggings of her rider's dress, she waded into the pool of water. When she entered the water at knee height, she stopped and stared at her toes wiggling clearly below the surface. Lucky and Elissa remained at the water's edge and watched her. Deeply absorbed in her own thoughts, Nest stood motionless.

"What are you looking for?" Lucky asked from the water's edge.

"If I knew, then I'd tell you. Maybe a spark of life," she answered turning and facing them. "It has all happened so fast. Everything seems so serious that it is not fun anymore."

"Here, catch this," Elissa said. "I grabbed some fruit from the Boab Tree for lunch. See what you think."

Nest gloved the flying fruit with her hands and began peeling the skin. She took a small sample of the pulp and savored it. A new sense of life flooded her countenance and she began to kick her feet in the water, splashing small waves around her legs. She glanced at the top of the gorge surrounding the crystal blue-green pool. A small bird took flight from the Boab Tree on the cliff's edge. Her body turned to track its flight over the water.

Having made a decision inside her soul, she announced, "Let's drop the Middle East and go to the surviving Dragon flyers at the base of the Himalayas. We'll take them the essence of the Boab Tree."

She moved and faced Lucky for his response.

He smiled at her, "OK. Take me back to the church in Patara."

Nest strolled out of the water toward Lucky. "The Boab essence needs another hour to solarize." Lying down on the sandy beach, Nest closed her eyes as she told him, "Rest up and enjoy the sun while you can."

He followed her suggestion, sitting down on the beach beside her. Appreciating the warmth and the lush scenery, he nodded. "Let me guess. Kuan Yin is with the survivors at the base camp in the Himalayas. She is the goddess of compassion."

"We need to have compassion for ourselves," she surrendered. "The survivors haven't given up. They are still players in this game of life."

Chapter Six

Nest left Lucky on the snow-covered steps of the church. The town was still vacant, except for a few Elves restoring the greenery in Town Square. After saying goodbye, she softly kissed him on the lips. Lucky returned her gesture with a passionate embrace.

"May we have some of your Elves to help spruce up the Rhakotis Library?" she asked in a seductive whisper. He overwhelmed her with his fervor. Clinging to Nicholas like a long lost lover, she desired a remembrance from him. In her present hormonal state of mind, Nest would have asked him for his tunic, but it seemed cumbersome and inappropriate. She still felt businesslike with him, despite where her mission might take her. So she settled on the Elves, who were more than willing to share their knowledge.

"Oh sure, anything," he gasped, holding her tightly.

"OK, kids," Elissa announced. "Time to go. Destiny calls."

"Oh yes, you are right," Nest realized as she reluctantly withdrew.

"Are you married?" Lucky asked.

"I am not in a committed relationship, though the King of Powyrs is my young, faithful companion," Nest replied, touching her flushed cheek as she glanced at the snow underneath her feet. She raised her head and turned toward him again. "If you ask me, there's nothing official. I want my freedom, which is why I am interested in the Boab Tree. I don't want to be defined as the queen of some king or the queen of some universe, especially if that place is in a big mess. All you have is the queen of some mess. Let's first clean things up a bit. Then I might be more proactive about accepting an official title, one that I can be proud of. I want a destiny that is congruent with my spiritual identity."

"Me too," he admitted.

"I'll call you Nicholas from now on," she said. "Maybe you and I are together so that we can define each other. It is like looking at the moon for a reflection and casting away shadows. The world is very lucky to have your help."

"Ahem," Elissa interrupted them. "There is no time to waste. The town inhabitants will return soon and rebuild their lives in Patara. With Nicholas around, the Byzantines will not attack again. He knows how to work the system."

"Nicholas. It's my name for now," he answered as he lifted her to Elissa's back. "I'll send a few Elves to Rhakotis Library to cheer up the place and organize the stacks. They love doing things like that."

"Thank you," she said as she almost fell off Elissa with another attempted kiss.

Elissa straightened and Nicholas gently pushed Nest back onto the dragon. He patted Nest on her back, gently lowering his head against Elissa's scales. Then he securely strapped her to the dragon's back in a similar manner that she had done for him earlier. Nest closed her eyes with understanding as he tightened the lines. As her passenger lapsed into a light daze, Elissa extended her great golden wings.

"I understand human nature," he told Nest. "Keep in touch."

Nicholas watched Elissa soar high in the white clouds before entering his church. He noticed the evergreen boughs and tinsel that the Elves had used for decoration on the tomblike stonewalls. For the first in a long while, the place felt much brighter and light. *If the Druids could find enlightenment in their hard, stone castles*, he thought, *then these new castle-like churches could fulfill spiritual intentions.*

"What do you think about the new look?" a small Elf, who had quietly appeared from behind a tree loaded with ornaments, asked.

"It's beautiful, Wanda," he told her. "You have brought the nature spirits back into the castle for protection. It will save all of our souls."

"Thank you," Wanda replied.

"Put some greenery in the steeple dome," he suggested. "This is one of the few churches built without an implant or a skeletal fragment from a loved one. I saw to that."

"I remember running that operation," she recalled. "We were meant for greater things. Speaking of which, where is Queen Nest going now?"

Nicholas sat down on the bench of the last pew. To the Druids, he would always be known as Lucky, but now that he was in a church, his constituents referred to him as Nicholas. He bowed his head and ran his fingers through his hair in understated angst. Rubbing his hands over his eyes, he told her, "She is off to the Himalayas. The last Serpentine attack left a prion in the minds of the survivors. She is bringing the Boab essence to them."

"She knows what she is missing by leaving," Wanda comforted him. "It must be painful for her to confront the devastation. She likes you because you are the one other person in the world who understands the gravity of her mission."

"Yes, I purposely left her in daze," he admitted. "She knows that she inspires me. By the time she regains full consciousness, she'll be able deal with the trauma."

"It will help with the resistance to the prion," Wanda surmised. "Stress destroys immunity."

"Yes, I know," he answered. "Hopefully, she can stop the spread before we all lose our minds. Witnessing the continued tragedy will make us crazy. We all have our limits. Let me be the first to admit that. Love and desire can have analgesic effects, which if used wisely can work wonders. The man who presently pursues her doesn't perceive the desperate situation in the universe in the same way that we do. We are crazy about each other because we understand without having to waste words explaining the problem. There is a physical attraction, which I won't deny. Having similar rings serves to encourage the partnership. We are so intrigued with the partnership that we are too focused for a prion to drive us crazy. Together we correct the imbalances and degradation in the template relationship between Adam and Lilith as well as Eve. Our focus is not technology or domination, rather we are obsessed with finding our freedom from the shackles have plagued human existence."

"Give it a rest, Nicholas. You stopped the source of the attacks at Basrah," Wanda said, sitting down next to the priest in the pew.

"Yes, we were successful. The partnership is a functional one, and we are not wrong to pursue it for all it is worth. The region will be known as Al-Basrah now," he added looking up. "Though, I think that the Hindoos are in for a long haul with the Serpentine attacks. It is going to take at least a thousand years to turn this around."

"The Celts are in for a long haul, too," Wanda added, gently putting her arm around Nicholas. "Carolus Magnus destroyed Nest's ancestral home in Germany. Her Saxon cousins there were all killed. There are a few relations left in England, but they have all gone underground. Carolus Magnus spoke to the Arabs and inspired the assault on the Noris base, which is in the Himalayas," Wanda remarked. "The Noris arrived in Atlantis with severe spiritual wounds. There was only one survivor from the Serpentine attack. He brought them in with the help of their sponsors, who eventually became lost in their egos and turned into gods."

****

While Wanda and Nicholas discussed the latest events of the Western world, Nest landed in the Indus Valley.

"I need a drink," she said as she surveyed the damaged temple, dead bodies, and burned homes. She wanted to escape the overwhelming sense of despair, if only in her mind. Something inside her revealed that she had reached her limit. "Where did the survivors go?"

"You need a steady boyfriend," Elissa corrected, whiffing the air. Her large dragon nostrils flared in the breeze. "I smell survivors lying half-dead in a cave several miles away."

"Forget the boyfriend," Nest retorted, finding her composure by surrendering to the moment. "The complications of the world mirror my love life. Let's get out of here before we get busted."

"First, we must burn the dead Sea Dragons. They were my brothers and sisters," she admitted. "We must follow the code of honor. Hide the evidence under duress."

"Oh right. Of course," Nest said, bowing her head in respect. A tremor ran through her body like a shock wave. Elissa's words centered her, and she no longer felt like escaping. "Sorry."

Elissa rushed over to the carcasses left in the temple and began flaming them. Nest did her best to promote the fire, but Elissa proved more effective. Stepping back for a moment, the woman continued to watch the horizon. When she noticed a horde of Arab armies racing toward them like fire ants down a hill, she motioned for Elissa to hurry.

"We can leave quickly through the portal at the back of the temple ruins. All we have to do is move some fallen rock," Elissa instructed.

Nest agreed. "I'll play with the balance in the elements and blow some dragon smoke in their direction. It will give us some time while you roll some stones."

Nest hurried to the elemental grid in far right corner of the temple then she tapped one of the sections with her sword. A light breeze emerged from the surrounding mountains. It stirred the dust of the town and gathered strength. A gust merged with the smoke of the fire, feeding the flames until they leaped high in the air. A huge swirl of dark smoke and flames danced through the fallen village. Burning everything combustible in its path, the huge fireball gathered momentum until a thick cloud separated Nest and Elissa from the invaders.

"Well, it appears that the human form of the Serpentines is alive and well," Nest commented as she entered the portal with Elissa. "Whatever they failed to do in Atlantis, they have now achieved. Now their achievement is after us."

"Keep moving," Elissa encouraged. "We must keep moving."

Chapter Seven

After exiting the temple through the portal, they located the cave above the Indus Valley. Elissa continued to follow the scent of decaying bodies, and directed Nest to the cave. The end placed them only a few steps away from their destination. The proximity of the portal to the cave shielded them from view, so they could work undetected by the invaders in the valley.

"We've come to help you," Nest greeted as they entered the cave of survivors. She wanted to keep things light and casual to avoid alarming the inhabitants.

A dying man wearing a turban lifted his hand and waved feebly. Nest quickly removed the Boab essence from her travel pouch. She placed two drops in a flask of water and briskly swirled it in her right hand. Kneeling next to the man, she moistened his lips with the fluid. His eyes fluttered wide open and he began coughing out black phlegm. Nest quickly got out of the way of the projectile spit. She administered the concoction to the others in the cave. Of the twelve people in the cave, two were already dead. The rest began to revive with the Boab essence.

"I think that I am done here. Where's the water supply?" she asked Elissa.

"We are not quite finished yet. Their drinking water is over there," she said pointing a scaled finger at a large vase.

"Let's check it out," Nest said.

Nest immediately drew a sample without touching the water with her skin. She put the sample in a vial and capped it. Racing to the opening of the cave, she extracted a leaf from a nearby bush. The young woman removed the cap of the vial and placed a drop on a leaf lying on the floor. The leaf quickly deteriorated as the droplet of water penetrated the surface. A painful thought surfaced as she recognized the poisoned water. Rushing over to the vase, she examined the symbols etched in the clay.

"Here's the problem," she told Elissa. "There's a symbol with an eye inside a triangle. Nobody looked closely at the design. It is very tiny, but it is there. It's the eye in the sky."

"There must have been some infiltration by the Serpentines," Elissa commented. "These people must be moved to safety."

"How about Mount Arbudaanchal?" she asked. "The Gurjars can protect them during the war between Celestials and demons."

"Great idea," Elissa agreed. Turning toward a figure that had suddenly appeared at the entrance to the cave. Elissa recognized the immortal, who often appeared unexpectedly in far away places at convenient moments. The golden Sea Dragon queen greeted her, "Hello, Kuan Yin. Glad that you could meet us. These Noris are in very bad shape."

"I know. They will need a place to safely recover. Mount Arbudaanchal will be a very good place for them," Kuan Yin, who was both a goddess and time traveler, said as she entered the cave and hugged Elissa. "Some of the Celestials from the Sun star settled there instead of China. The Gurjars are very fierce warriors."

"You are just the goddess that we need. Hello, Kuan Yin," Nest said as she ran to embrace the time traveler. "Nicholas was happy to receive the golden tara."

"Do you mean Lucky?" Kuan Yin asked.

"Yes," Nest laughed softly, ignoring the devastating circumstances in light of the goddess of compassion. Then she remembered her mission. "He's known as Nicholas now. He will be pope someday."

"I guess a Pope by the name of Lucky won't be as appreciated as a Pope Nicholas," Kuan Yin mused.

"Yes. They like celebrating Christmas over there," Nest commented. "It is so cold and desolate that they search to find something to celebrate. If he was at the Hill of Tara, I think that Pope Lucky would be a more popular name."

Kuan Yin smiled at the reviving Hindoos, who stared at the goddess of compassion with wide eyes. "Some Chinese Dragon flyers will carry you to Mount Arbudaanchal. We have notified the Gurjars, who will take you in as Chauhans. You can retain your identity and help maintain the balance for the planet."

The man with the turban fainted with happiness. The other ten people in the cave asked for food and water. Nest produced some supplies from Elissa's pouch and passed around some samples. It was important that the survivors eat small portions so that they wouldn't become sick.

"The Noris are from the Centaurus Galaxy," Kuan Yin began. "The Serpentines exploded their galaxy and the Noris's soul fragments were shuttled to Atlantis. There was only one survivor and he reassembled the fragments. Unfortunately, some Serpentines got caught in the mix and infiltrated Atlantis. They succeeded in getting the governing board to pass the Atlantean Treaty with the Serpentines."

Nest rolled her eyes and slapped her head with her hand. "Is that how they got that passed? It was the stupidest thing that ever happened."

"An Atlantean named Faust made a deal with a Reptilian in the mix," Kuan Yin revealed. "The rest is history."

"You cannot deal with the devil," Nest insisted. "I always wondered about the truth of Atlantis's collapse."

"That reminds me. We need to upgrade the gridding for protection. Do you have the green diamond for the Four Directions grid?" Kuan Yin asked the survivors.

A woman nodded and pointed to the turban on the head of the man who had passed out. Kuan Yin unraveled the cloth around his head and exposed the green crystal diamond. It rolled to the ground, landing in the sand with a light thud that awoke the man.

"Thank you," Kuan Yin softly told the man as he blinked his eyes open. Noticing Kuan Yin pick up the green diamond from the ground, he smiled sweetly.

Several Dragon flyers from China arrived at the entrance of the cave. A man wearing a white tunic appeared with them. He directed the flyers to the recovering Chauhans on the floor of the cave.

"Hi, Emaile," Kuan Yin greeted warmly. "I haven't seen you for a while."

"Been busy in the Celestial realm," he replied. "When I heard about the attack on the on the Indus Valley, I dropped everything immediately. I have a message to bring you."

"What is it?" Nest asked.

"We must grid the green diamond in the site of the original Four Directions. Things have shifted and there is new information coming."

"Just what I thought. That means that we must go through the MidEarth," Kuan Yin commented.

"Yes," Emaile said. "Hurry. We need the gridding restored as soon as possible."

Nest held the hand of man with the turban gently and said goodbye. Then she waved to the rest of the survivors as the Dragon flyers prepared them for their flight to Mount Arbudaanchal. Emaile left the cave and disappeared in the morning sun.

"How do we get to the Four Directions grid?" Nest asked.

"Through a portal in the MidEarth," Elissa said.

"How do we get to the MidEarth now that Utopia has been shut off?" Nest questioned.

"Glastonbury Tor," Elissa replied as Nest hugged Kuan Yin goodbye.

****

The trip to the site of the Four Directions grid took almost a day. Nest wasn't so eager to revisit Glastonbury Tor, though several hundred years had passed since the Serpentines attacked the abbey. Trauma still hung in the air, while they seared for the portal to the MidEarth. It would take another hundred years to clear the atmosphere. Glastonbury Tor had been built over the ruins of the Flowery Meadow, which was the headquarters for the Pink Knights. The knights restored Avalon after the Serpentines destroyed it during the reign of King Cole, King Arthur's great-grandfather. According to Druid history, it often took three attempts before an operation achieved success.

After they found it, they journeyed through the MidEarth, and revived their sagging spirits. They entered the Singing Cave from the portal in the MidEarth and hiked on foot to the grid. Nest found the indentation for the green diamond and inserted it. There was enough ambient light in the cave to show light through the crystal. The crystal's reflection created several images on the wall of the Singing Cave. Nest gasped at the illuminations. Taking a deep breath, she sat down on the floor studied them carefully. "The Boab Tree replaces the Tree of Knowledge in the planetary grid," she observed. "Apparently, the Tree of Knowledge served as a decoy."

"Yes, the seven Celestial Founding systems sensed that a Tree of Knowledge would attract a Serpentine influence," Elissa explained.

"Who removed the green diamond after Queen Joslin placed it in the Four Directions grid?" Nest questioned.

"Queen Creirwy," Elissa answered. "She figured out that the Tree of Knowledge had been a decoy and took the green diamond to the civilization at the Indus Valley. She needed the Noris to reconfigure it."

"How?" Nest questioned.

"She needed their tears," Elissa explained. "It was the first step to healing their wounded souls."

"Creirwy ran out of time and couldn't retrieve it," Nest observed. "The tears mark the rite of passage for the Kingdom of Tara."

"Yes, she and Tinka ascended in a hurry to run interference," Elissa said. "It brought the civilization in the Indus Valley more time to escape."

Chapter Eight

"The Four Directions grid has been restored," Nest said as she impatiently tapped her foot for moment. Throwing her arms in the air, she quickly decided something. "I want to go back home to the Hill of Tara."

"Spend the night with the Four Directions grid to settle the energy," Elissa advised as she joined Nest on the floor of the cave, curling her body in a sleepy, catlike pose. "Tomorrow we can leave for home." The Sea Dragon queen languidly closed her eyes and continued in a soft, ominous whisper. "You'll need your rest before returning to the Hill of Tara."

"Huh?" Nest asked in a dumbfounded state of alarm. After their recent mission concerning the prion survivors, the tone of the Sea Dragon's words seemed eerie. *Was the Hill of Tara threatened?* Hypersensitive to Elissa's innuendo, Nest could not imagine the reason to remain. She knew that Elissa was a master of the understatement, and trusted her. By the time Elissa's final words registered in Nest's consciousness, the Sea Dragon had drifted into a deep sleep. Realizing that it was fruitless to question Elissa further, Nest arranged her bedroll on the floor of the cave and examined the designs again. Now she couldn't sleep. Something in the new images bothered her. Eventually she drifted into a half-sleep with various images appearing in her consciousness like shooting stars. The visualizations faded too quickly for her to grasp their entire meaning.

The next day she woke and placed her travel pack in Elissa's pouch. After hiking to the entrance of the Singing Cave, Nest hurriedly climbed onto the back of the golden Sea Dragon queen. Now that they had found the Four Directions grid, they could exit through the cave's opening. People could only find the Four Directions grid by entering through the MidEarth. This one-way invisibility shield prevented intruders from finding the Four Directions grid either by accident or purposeful malice.

"I have a feeling that something is amiss at the Hill of Tara," Nest told Elissa as they soared beyond the clouds. After having desired to go immediately home last night, her instincts told her otherwise. The Sea Dragon's concerns last night continued to resonate with her. Nest decided that she needed to find the cause for alarm before continuing.

"I sense it too. The issue is still there from last night. I'm glad you got your rest," Elissa responded as she flew higher and higher above the clouds. "We'll land in Mercia instead."

"Great idea, especially now that Beowulf is gone," Nest agreed. "That displaced Dane gave Alfie's daughter a hard time."

"She drove the Grays out of Mercia," Elissa remarked. "Alfie would be proud."

They landed in a shire near Stafford where Nest left Elissa to forage while she inquired in the village about the local news. Traumatized by what she had witnessed in the Indus Valley, Nest reasoned that she would be quite happy if she never met a Gray or Serpentine. Cautiously, she inquired in town for news about the Hill of Tara.

"Merfyn is claiming to be the next King of Gwynedd," a woman told her. "He intends to force his way into the Kingdom of Powys."

With this information Nest quickly thanked the woman and left town in search of her wandering Sea Dragon. She followed the road out of the shire and searched the forest. Fortunately, no one had found the Sea Dragon and created panic in the village, otherwise Nest would have wasted precious time in crowd control. She felt as lonely and afraid as she did when she left Nicholas in frozen Patara.

"They are already united," Nest told Elissa after she found her Sea Dragon munching on a fern in the local forest.

"He is using your absence as an opportunity to insert himself into the lineage," Elissa acknowledged.

"What do we do now?" she asked, feeling nauseated at the thought of going down in Druid history as the queen of a traitor.

"Marry him," she suggested.

"What?" Nest almost screamed. She felt alarmed at the kind of advice that everyone, except Nicholas, readily supplied. Everyone, good and bad, wanted to define her.

"On paper only," Elissa proposed.

"There you are," her lover, Elise, interrupted. He made his way through the forest understory. He pulled back a few branches and appeared before Nest. "I saw you flying overhead."

"Elise, we were just talking about you," Nest interjected as she turned around to address him. "Elissa thinks that I should marry Merfyn."

"Well, that would be a quite a ploy," Elise told her as he swept her in his arms.

Nest allowed herself to be carried away without any more distractions. If her mission with Nicholas felt complicated, her life with Elise seemed almost too simple. She realized that freedom was not obtained through a single mission; it had to be cultivated and guarded. Like Nicholas, she concluded that she could not ignore her past or escape her destiny. In their own way, Elise and Merfyn were just other loose ends to tie up. For Merfyn, hopefully the outcome would be severance, whereas Elise constituted a beginning.

"The next heir will be my child," he promised.

"What do we do about Merfyn?" she asked him.

"Send him away to fight Pepin in Aquitaine," he told Nest before kissing her deeply.

"Now, that's a great idea," Nest heavily breathed. "How will we ever pull it off?"

"Leave it to me," he answered. "The Roman Britons already consider me to be your brother."

"That is what happens when you hang around my father for extended periods of time," she replied.

"Someone had to put in a good word for you," he said. "The Stone of Destiny skipped his generation."

"He's not complaining," Nest reminded him.

"Neither am I," he told her. "We all have a job to do. I'll bring the papers to Merfyn myself."

"How will we get him off to Aquitane *before* the honeymoon?" she questioned him.

"We'll elicit your Father's help," Elise replied. "He is still the King of Gwynedd."

"What would your great-grandfather, Patrick, say about this?" Nest jested.

"He'd approve. He made all those monasteries for his children," Elise said.

"Take me back to the Hill of Tara," she demanded, suddenly aware that others had more control over her destiny than she did. Her time with Nicholas had given her a taste of freedom and self-determination. She had just returned from a dangerous mission on promoting gender balance, and now she could not even legally represent herself in the Roman Empire.

"Not until we sidetrack Merfyn Frych, the other man who wants to marry you," he responded.

Nest glanced at Elissa, who nodded at her. "All right," she consented. "I'll hang out in the Kingdom of Powys while you and Dad get the paperwork together. The Briton Serpentines adore paperwork."

"Once Merfyn is off to Aquitaine, we can start making the next heir," he proposed.

"What if Merfyn finds out?" she asked.

"He won't. He doesn't like sex," he told her.

"How do you know?" she asked.

"He's hung up on his adopted patron, Esyllst, sometimes known as Morgasia, depending on which country one travels. He knows that he will get nowhere with this loveless witch. That's why he stays with her; he doesn't want a relationship," he replied. "Like most Roman Britons, he doesn't like women. That's why they never recognize women as heirs. Instead they entertain their mothers, who vicariously live through them."

'That's also why it makes it easy to pull a fast one on him," she said thoughtfully.

"Young men like me never let women out of our sight," he confessed.

"Is that how you were able to find me in the middle of a forest in Mercia?" she joked.

"Yes," he confessed. Then he picked her up, turned around, and began carrying her to another village. "Come with me to Winchcombe Abbey."

"Oh, you make such a great pair, I should have directed Nest to Nicholas sooner." Elissa sighed.

"We had to regroup to protect the new Queen of the Universe," Elise mentioned. "Nicholas has more experience than I with women, though he has also had more difficulties than I with women."

"Nicholas makes everyone feel lucky," Nest rejoined. "It was just what we needed to get passed the complications."

Elissa sauntered after the happy couple, while occasionally pausing to feast on wild edibles. She followed closely behind until Elise stopped at the main road. He stopped for a second and put Nest back down on the ground. After taking a deep breath, he whistled loudly. A stallion emerged from a stable across the road. The horse trotted toward its rider and remained steady while Elise lifted Nest to its back.

"Meet me at the Dragon stalls," he instructed Elissa. "We'll ride to Winchcombe Abbey on horseback so that the Briton Serpentines don't notice us. Then you and I will fly to Powys to arrange the paperwork with King Cadell. The less connected Nest remains to this subterfuge, the better."

"I'll be waiting for you at Winchcombe Abbey," Elissa promised as she extended her great wings and flew into the sun.

"Bring my father to Winchcombe Abbey," Nest told him. "I want to see him before he registers me with the Briton Roman authorities."

"Don't worry," he assured her as the stallion raced down the road. "Merfyn will never see you again."

Chapter Nine

When they reached Winchcombe Abbey, Elise left Nest at a cottage near the monastery. She immediately began turning the place into a home. Although, she felt mild ecstasy at the thought of spending the rest of her life with Elise, someone with whom she already spent most of her life, the recognition that she was still a fugitive from Roman law and history filled her with self doubt. She could yield her sword in Turkey and the Middle East, but had to use strategy and cunning to obtain her goals in Europe. It was a different fight. This notion frightened and caused her sorrow, but as she told herself, *at least I am not dead like my ancestors*, even if their battles were more obvious and well-defined. Her freedom was found in her ability to choose her response to the injustices surrounding her. Like Nicholas, she had chosen to work within the system, though she never gave it her allegiance.

Meanwhile, Elise raced to the Dragon stalls to confer with Elissa. He was so happy for his moment in history, where he could have the woman he loved while out-foxing competitors to his throne. Without love, souls shriveled and died. Merfyn would do the same as long as he didn't tie up his opponent's passions in a struggle. He had found heaven, whereas Merfyn was headed for oblivion, existing on only paper that would be eventually forgotten or erased.

"There you are," the young man said as he spied Elissa behind a low wall.

"A little more shine on the backside," she commented to her caretaker. Then she addressed the young man. "Oh, Elise! Are you ready for a little bureaucratic nonsense?"

"Anything for love," he airily replied. "Let's go visit King Cadell and tell him that I am marrying his daughter to someone else so that I can be with her."

Cadell and Elise arranged the paperwork to make it appear that Nest had legally married Merfyn. Then her father returned with Elise to see Nest at Winchcombe Abbey. She met them in the stalls dismounting from their Sea Dragons.

"The deed is done," King Cadell told his daughter with a mighty hug. "Merfyn doesn't care about what you do with your private life. He doesn't even know where you are. The marriage certificate is just an empty piece of legal paper." Facing the young man next to him, he added, "On the day the Stone of Destiny chose Nest, I always knew that you two were meant for each other. Be her life partner. Bless you both."

The presence of her father reassured her. Together, the three planned the future.

****

Nine months later, Nest gave birth to a beautiful baby boy. She called him Rhodri, which was short for the English form of Roderick. Elise was jubilant about the success of the operation.

"He's going to be great!" he teased as he swiped the infant from her arms and danced with him around the room. "I am so happy that you two are cooperating with my plan to preserve the Kingdom of the Golden Tara."

Exhausted from the delivery, Nest merely smiled and closed her eyes for a light sleep.

"We know who the power is behind the throne," he told his newborn son. Rhodri responded with a hearty wail.

"It is him,"Nest said, opening her eyes and reaching for her baby.

Elise handed him to her so Rhodri could nurse. The baby immediately quieted and suckled her breast. Meanwhile, a golden dragon snout nudged the window slightly ajar. Nest looked up from her content infant to the familiar face in the open window.

"There is another mission coming," Elissa interrupted. "Rest up."

"What?" Nest exclaimed. "We just got done with this one."

"Give it a month or two," Elissa suggested.

"Maybe *six*. I want to take the baby to the Hill of Tara," Nest decided. "I want to introduce him to his grandparents while Merfyn spends time with distant relations in Aquitaine."

"One other thing," Elissa began, cocking her head from side to side. "I don't know how to break this to you, but Ceredigion has been given to the Collas of Airghialla."

"Well, there goes the neighborhood," Elise commented.

"They were the ones that Patrick chased from the Hill of Tara," Nest added. "Their mother fled to Scotland and roomed with the King of Alba."

"Kenny is putting his kingdom underground in the same manner as his grandfather Fergie did," Elissa said. "I heard about it from Gilderoy."

"When were you visiting Gilderoy?" Nest asked. Gidleroy was a revolutionary Sea Dragon presently taking on the dark forces in Scotland.

"I took a short trip to Scotland while you were in labor," Elissa confessed. "You will need to visit those Scottish rebels, too."

"There is a difference between the Kingdom of Alba and the Kingdom of Dal Riata," Elise acknowledged. "Kenny walks a fine line."

"Soon it will be hidden by Roman legalities," Nest answered. "According to the Stone of Destiny, the leadership of Scotland goes to his daughter, Mael Muire."

"The Latin authorities will record the King of Alba's sons as the rulers of Scotland," Elise projected. "It is only paperwork. After everything that has occurred on Scottish soil, no one will ever accept a ruler named Constantine, except for the Roman Britons. No true leader in the United Kingdom would *ever* call a son by that name. The offspring recorded by the Roman bureaucracy are not Kenny's. His sons are being educated at the Hill of Tara."

"Where are you going with this?" Elissa inquired.

"I don't know," Nest thoughtfully replied. "I really don't care about all this bloodline business. Rich or poor, it turns people into a commodity."

"The Stone of Destiny cuts through all the red tape," Elise agreed. "Who cares? The best leaders are not chosen by blood or inheritance, but other qualities that often remain imperceptible to the locals. That is what is so exciting about the process. It is meaningful."

"We just play their games enough to stay alive," Nest said. "At least we have the Kingdom of the Golden Tara. They cannot take our tears away from us. Sorrow cuts us from Roman legions more decisively than the use of violence."

"What else can we do?" Elise posed rhetorically.

Elissa rolled her eyes with a sigh. "Thrive. I'll come back later when the baby is old enough to travel."

"See you later," Elise said with a wave of his hand. As usual, the wisdom of the golden Sea Dragon queen had triumphed over his limited viewpoint. He remained intently focused on his lover and son. "Say hello to Gilderoy and the others on your next vacation in Scotland."

****

Six months later, Nest strapped her infant to her breast and climbed on Elissa's back.

"He is so cute," she told the golden Sea Dragon queen. "He is ready for his first Sea Dragon flight."

"Say hello to your Mom and Dad," Elise told her before Elissa spread her great wings. "Let them know that I am keeping a watch on things so that little Rhodri has his own kingdom."

"I will," she beamed at him.

Moments later, Elissa, Nest, and little Rhodri landed at Rath Grannes. Her parents met her there and helped her dismount. Nest handed Rhodri to her mother and hugged them all at once.

"We sent Merfyn packing when we heard about the pregnancy," Patty told Nest. "His birth officially displaces Merfyn's reign. Rhodri will be safe growing up at the Hill of Tara."

"What do you think about that, little Rhodri?" King Cadell cooed.

A soft coo echoed throughout the land. It was sound coming from the Stone of Destiny, heralding the future King Roderick. They all looked around. Rhodri quieted with an air of smug contentment. Though he might become listed in the Roman history books as the son of Merfyn, he would successfully restore the throne of his biological parents.

"Well, it appears that we have confirmation from the Stone of Destiny," King Cadell commented. "I didn't know that the Stone of Destiny could speak baby talk."

"Simple lives, complicated times," Nest reasoned. "Elise stayed in Mercia to keep watch on Northumbria."

"Here we are keeping an eye on the Kingdom of Airghialla," Patty remarked.

"In Scotland, they are sidestepping the Kingdom of Alba," Nest rejoined.

"We must finish shielding the Kingdom of the Golden Tara," Patty said, taking the infant from her life partner. "We must become even more transparent to the Serpentines. The attack on the Glastonbury Tor hundreds of years ago showed us the problem with living too close to those without the same values."

"We only have until the turn of the next century," King Cadell agreed.

"What is going to happen then?" Nest questioned.

"The Serpentines will most likely have their own network in place," he surmised. "I heard that they are calling themselves *Illuminati* and they want to rebuild Jerusalem in their own image. They have established a base at the priory."

"What do you suggest that we do with the Hill of Tara?" Nest questioned. "Can you think of anymore loose ends? Might as well mix business with pleasure."

"Leave that it up to Elissa," King Cadell replied.

"What makes you say that?" Nest asked.

Patty grinned, "The Stone of Destiny says to expect more Dragon eggs. A new generation of Dragon flyers is coming. There must be hope."

"What?" Nest cried, wrinkling her brow in amazement. "Elise and I made her take a vacation."

Overhearing their conversation, Elissa blushed. Nest turned toward her and stroked her shiny gold scales. Elissa turned a brighter shade of red.

"Who is the lucky dragon?" she asked the golden Sea Dragon queen.

"Curtis." She sighed. "It happened quickly in Scotland. Gilderoy set me up."

"What ever happened to Ivan?" Nest asked.

"Dragons don't mate for life," she admitted. "We have long lives and swim around too much. It would never be practical to remain with the same dragon for hundreds of years."

"Oh," Nest said, trying to imagine the fickle love life of a Sea Dragon.

"I still love Ivan, too," Elissa insisted airily. "I can never forget what we had together, but Ivan has been busy for the past four hundred years in Northern England. We only see each other in passing. Curtis, well, he was *available*, and my clock was ticking."

"Forget the details," Patty offered. "Let's party! We'll find those Dragon eggs later."

"Give it another eight months," Elissa admitted. "The nest has been timed with Rhodri's development. I always wanted another toddler. I remember that Gerwyn was so much fun."

Chapter Ten

"Where's your Dragon lover now?" Nest asked the golden Sea Dragon queen.

"He's nesting the eggs with Gilderoy and Pailsey," Elissa replied. "He and the guys are busy."

Placing her hands on her hip, Nest continued to confront Elissa, "Somehow I have the feeling that I am not as in tune with you as my predecessors."

"True, but you got Dragon eggs from me faster than any one else," Elissa assured her. "I should hang out with a twenty-one year old more often."

"Hmm, maybe it did work out for the best," Nest realized as she waved her parents off with the baby.

Rhodri and his grandparents seemed eager to leave Nest and Elissa alone. It was a tender moment between flyer and dragon. Nest handed Cadell a bag with things for the baby. She pointed out several containers of breast milk in one of the compartments.

"I extracted reserve milk for Rhodri," she said. "This discussion could take awhile. I intend to get to the bottom of it. My dragon has not been very forthcoming with critical information." She turned to Elissa. "Where are the eggs?" she questioned.

"Petra," she said.

"Jordan?" Nest almost shouted. "When did you go to Petra, Jordan? It not only is one of the seven wonders of the world, but Petra is a Blue's base!"

"Curtis and I wandered over to Petra to see what the wonder was all about," Elissa related dreamily. "Next thing we knew, we were in Petra. The Dragon eggs just happened. What a wonder!"

"Let me guess—one thing led to another?" Nest speculated.

"How did you know?" Elissa asked rather innocently.

"Never mind. Let's stay focused," Nest answered. "When do you need to get back to the nest?"

"Six months," she replied as she counted on her fingers-like claws.

"That's a lot of time," Nest remarked. "What is Curtis like? I don't believe I have met him."

"He's a white-eared Sea Dragon from the Indus Valley. He came with the batch from Miriah's well in Egypt, the one that the locals believe is haunted," Elissa said. "Miriah is the ghost who taught the white-eyed Dragons how to inhabit the multidimensional world. They had to go behind the veil to find her. It was sorta like hide-and-seek."

"A surviving dragon?" Nest gasped.

"No, he saw it coming," Elissa said. "He wanted to join Gilderoy's and Pailsey's rebellion in Scotland instead."

"Why didn't the others listen?" Nest questioned.

"Well, you know how it is," she explained. "Let playing dragons play."

"What? You mean that the Sea Dragons were too busy fooling around to notice what was about to land on them?" Nest asked, growing impatient and angry.

"Yes," Elissa said succinctly. "It is the nature of the beast."

"How about adding a little common sense to the beast's nature?" Nest asked. "How about some focus or survival skills?"

"They didn't think about that," Elissa simply said. "They were busy playing."

"I see," Nest said. "They were contenders for the Darwin award."

"What's that?" she asked.

"Later." Nest laughed. Everyone knew that she had been gifted with pre-science. "I'm getting ahead of my time."

"Have it your way," Elissa responded.

Taking a deep breath, Nest continued. "I'm glad that you came through for me."

"Curtis too," Elissa added. "It takes two. Sometimes three."

"Yes, it does," Nest agreed as she put her arm around her Sea Dragon. Elissa's lack of concern for the foolhardy Sea Dragons that perished bothered her. Recalling Elissa's pain at the burial of the Sea Dragons during the rescue of the prion survivors, Nest didn't understand her fatalistic point of view. "Tell me more about this Curtis fellow. He seems advanced."

"He is." Elissa sighed. "Curtis calls me Spike."

"I see," Nest said. "Does he teach how to fight? Do you two dance and play with each other like we do?"

"Yes," she answered. "How did you know? Do you and Elise go 'round and 'round?"

"Don't worry about us," Nest replied, quickly changing the subject. "I've obviously been an influence. Let me guess, you also took out the local rulers in Alba."

"They attacked first," said Elissa.

"I am sure they did," Nest soothed. "Thank you for taking care of yourself. It will buy us time. We need to fortify our position before Alba gets greedy and plans a takeover."

"What do you mean?" Elissa questioned.

"Never mind," Nest replied. "Let's get you over to your caretaker for grooming. You must be exhausted. I must go check on how my parents are doing with Rhodri."

She waved for a caretaker to escort Elissa to the Dragon stalls. A young man walking in the far meadow saw her gesture and hurried toward her. Nest took a deep breath, noticing the subtle scent of wildflowers. She could not help but smell the freshness in the air. Leaving Elissa in the hands of her caretaker, Nest headed toward the suite where she knew that she could find her parents and Rhodri. She entered the corridor that led to their room. A soft baby's cry could be heard echoing in the empty hall. Stopping at the door, she recognized the voice of her infant before knocking. Patty, his grandmother, opened the door and handed the baby to Nest with a smile.

"He wants his mama," her mother laughed. "Nothing else will do."

Nest entered the room. She began nursing Rhodri in a chair by the hearth. Rhodri quieted as he hungrily sought her breast. While he nursed, Nest reflected on her discussion with Elissa.

"How did it go with Elissa and her new family?" her father asked, pulling up a chair next to hers.

"We bonded," she announced. "I never thought that I would have anything in common with a golden-scaled fighting mama, but I do now."

Patty chuckled softly as she sat down next to Cadell. She said, "It is all very exciting. There is always something profound about Sea Dragon eggs. The difficulty lies in determining the correct meaning. Usually, there is some follow up with gridding or alchemy."

"I don't think I have the depth of experience for this," Nest confessed. "Creirwy was much more seasoned."

"No, we needed someone fresh." Cadell smiled. "Aunt Creirwy continued to rebirth herself."

Recalling the freshness of the air that she had breathed near the meadow, Nest realized that her father was correct. Searching deep inside herself, Nest groped for any flicker of insight.

"The Dragon eggs are in Petra, Jordan," she started. "Elissa and Curtis were there on a hot date."

"What in Jordan would attract two Sea Dragons from Scotland?" her father questioned.

"It must have something to do with the intergalactic wars of ancient Egypt," Nest said as Rhodri fell asleep.

"How do you figure?" he asked.

"Curtis is a white-eared Sea Dragon from Miriah's well in Egypt. This means that he is skilled in interdimensional travel," Nest explained. "Their progeny will incorporate and build on the talents of their parents, if all goes well. Elissa produced invisible Sea Dragons with her last mate, who was very cat-like."

Patty rose from her chair and walked slowly toward a small window in the room. She gazed outside. Nest noticed a sudden revelation flash across her countenance.

"Carolus thanked us for removing the Grays from our land," she recalled. "Even he saw them as a threat. Though he would have conquered us if given half a chance, we were strong enough to fool him into thinking that we were his allies. Our transparency served us well. Now the time has come for a new tactic. We just don't know what that is yet."

"That is what bothers me," Nest admitted. "I can't see what the new tactic is yet, though I know that something fresh is needed.

Patty turned and smiled at Nest. "Maybe it has to do with the multi-dimensional bonding between you, Elise, and Nicholas."

Chapter Eleven

The next morning, Nest carried Rhodri over to the Dragon stalls to visit Elissa. They found the golden Sea Dragon queen enjoying a round of dragon's grog as she gossiped with the other Sea Dragons. It was a cool, crisp, early autumn day and a light wind was picking up over the meadow.

"Good morning," Elissa greeted. "How's little Rhodri?"

"Doing well. He's back on schedule," she reported. "Though, I can tell that he misses Elise."

"How are you doing?" Elissa asked.

"I don't know," she answered truthfully. "I feel fine, but something seems to be missing. If I could figure it out, I would correct it. I think that it has something to do with the new Dragon eggs."

"It has everything to do with the new Dragon eggs," Elissa told her. "You've lost a fragment of your soul. It reminds me of the time when the Serpentines destroyed the Noris's galaxy, and fragmented their souls. The escaped Noris had to resemble their souls in Atlantis, the refugee site. Unfortunately, a few Serpentines contaminated the mix."

"Is that it?" Nest exclaimed as she sat done on a bale of straw. "I knew that it was important, but what does this have to do with the new Dragon eggs?"

"I have seen many generations of Dragon flyers," she said. "This is the first generation that just seemed to be going through the motions. Compared to the others, your burden is relatively light. You are not fighting for your life every minute, like some of the others, nor are you being tortured to death."

"All the life has been sucked out of me," Nest rejoined. "I am already gone. It is as if I have been poisoned by contact with global desolation and despair.

I feel too exhausted to birth and oversee the next generation of Dragon flyers. The sight of the Dragon eggs moves me to tears."

"You are feeling overwhelmed by the enormity of your task, which is to put enough protection in place to guarantee soul survival in the dark ages. We must do something about that before the eggs hatch," she agreed.

"It is as if I never recovered from the trip to the Indus Valley," she reflected. "I feel so alone. Nothing seems to touch me anymore."

"Now you are getting it," Elissa said. "You must go back and heal the initial wounds that the Noris carried to Atlantis."

"How do I do that?" Nest asked.

"Get as much information as possible about their condition when they arrived," Elissa said.

"Where do I start?" she questioned. "That happened years ago."

"It's in the green diamond," Elissa told her. "You must look in its reflective flame."

"Does that mean that we must go back to the Four Directions grid in Singing Cave?" she asked.

"Eventually," Elissa replied. "You are too exhausted now and may even have some postpartum blues."

"Maybe," Nest said. "It was difficult to sidestep Merfyn and turn the tables on him. Sometimes I awake in a cold sweat, fearing that my plan will fail and that Merfyn will come for me."

"It is not over until he is gone," the golden Sea Dragon queen acknowledged.

"I get your point," she said. "The price that I pay for my freedom is a double life. I often deny there is jeopardy, but it really exists. I would be killed if my second life caught up with me."

"It is difficult to keep quiet when lives become complicated," Elissa pondered. "It is an accomplishment that deserves a pat on the back. Give yourself more credit."

"You just provided the answer," Nest realized, rising from her seat. Still carrying Rhodri as he slept, the young mother walked around the stall to stretch her legs. "I've tasted freedom and I want more. I yearn for wholeness and consistency. The foundation for the Kingdom of the Golden Tara is a rite of passage. The emptiness of loss must be traversed before getting to the other side of the issues."

"There's your answer to the problem of the Noris," Elissa elucidated.

"I suspect that they were not the only spirits that arrived damaged in Atlantis," she added. "Perhaps all of us have a condition that the Serpentine experimenters learned how to exploit. The more we heal, the less the Serpentines affect us. There's a non-violent solution for you."

"You got it," Elissa encouraged. "It is so complex that it is beyond my ability to explain."

"It was love that elicited the Noris's capacity to renew their spirit after they had been annihilated with their galaxy," Nest said.

"There is a black hole left from the destruction that can't be filled," Elissa said. "Both Noris and Serpentine get sucked into it."

"That's how the souls were transported to Atlantis," Nest surmised. "We need to correct the recovery process to keep the Serpentines out. This is why we must make ourselves transparent to the Serpentines. Besides refusing to operate at their level, we must fill in the hole with new constructs that vibrate at a higher frequency. In this manner, the souls become invisible to spiritual predators."

"This is exactly how the Serpentines came to Atlantis," Elissa said. "The black hole ends there."

"The Noris brought their enemies with them," Nest realized.

"The wounded souls matriculated in Greenland," Elissa observed. "Afterward, they went to their destinations on platforms. Some went to the west and some went east. Balance proved to be their best defense against Serpentine attacks."

"The question of balance runs deeper than east and west," Nest said.

"It is their deepest secret," Elissa revealed. "They bonded to each other's souls, like yin and yang."

"So two halves make a whole, but it is only a superficial bond," Nest said. "The survivors in the cave were in the process of reverting to their original condition, which was the state that their souls arrived in Greenland. They haven't healed that part of themselves."

"Yes," Elissa said. "When the Lemurian insurgents destroyed the Serpentine crystal, the soul injury was unmasked, as were the Serpentines, who had no souls."

"How do we plug the black hole so that no more Serpentines arrive?" Nest asked. Unsure of the effectiveness of transparency concept, she wanted more information. Elissa was a wellspring of ideas.

"You can't plug it, at least not with our current technology. You must use a filter," Elissa said. "The Serpentines are attracted to the light, but they cannot receive it. Shine the light on the Noris and they will retain it."

"Easier said than done," Nest said. "We'll need to put a lighting mechanism inside the black hole. Those spirits that can receive the light will pass through while those who miss the light will go by."

"We need the one who aided us on a similar case with the Atlantean exodus. His name is Emaile, a great spiritual warrior who often officiates at weddings. This Light Being also serves as an emissary to those hiding in the Himalayas," Elissa said. "He is the Celestial who can help us with this project. Emaile helped protect the Dragon flyers after they survived the sinking of Atlantis."

"How do we get a message to Emaile? It is easier to summon a spaceship than contact a time traveler directly. Emaile is a light being, which makes it even more problematic," Nest said.

"I'll call mom, Elissa decided. "The Noris called her Ea and put statues of her in their Asian palaces. She also helped the refugees flee Atlantis. Afterwards she was ready for a change and ascended. She serves as a specialist in these matters. Now that mom works in the Celestial realm, she can contact Emaile for us."

A man in a white tunic immediately appeared in the doorway of the stall. Nest quickly swirled around. Elissa lifted her head in pleasant surprise. He appeared radiant.

"Did you call for me?" Emaile asked.

"Yes, we did," Elissa said. Then she raised her head to the heavens and shouted, "Thanks, Mom!"

"We need a light filter in the black hole of the remaining Centaurus Galaxy," she said. "Can you throw one in there for us? We need to separate the Noris from the Serpentines."

"How about a light feed?" Emaile suggested. "We'll give it a continuous stream of light that we catch at the other end and recycle. The Noris should be able to grab hold, whereas it will slip through the fingers of the Serpentines."

"That should work," Nest responded. "What light source are you planning to use?"

"I think that I can string a few star fragments together," he replied. "It will be a long one, but there's plenty of material left in the Centaurus Galaxy."

"What happens to the entrapped Serpentines?" Nest asked.

"They'll get lost in their own black hole and dissipate," he told her.

"That should work very well." Nest nodded to Elissa. "How soon can you get on it?'

"With some help from a few Pegasi, it should take a month to get everything in place," Emaile calculated. "The cleanup operation will take no more than half a million years."

"Compared to geologic timing, that isn't so long," Nest acknowledged.

"I'll get on it right away," Emaile promised as he hurried into the rising sun.

Nest peered out of the doorway and watched him disappear over the horizon. Rhodri remained sleeping in his carrier. She looked down and gazed at his peaceful face. She felt amazed that she could bring anyone such contentment. Puzzling over the dynamics of the Noris soul retrieval system, Nest sensed that they achieved a similar enlightened state of bonding. Somehow, she must move them toward wholeness if they were to ever truly heal.

"We have more work to do," Nest told Elissa. "We must figure out how to grid this for everyone's benefit. The Noris may not be the only ones that arrived to the planet under these circumstances. I must do more research."

Chapter Twelve

"Here's the problem," Nest said as she closed one of the papyrus books. She glanced down at Rhodri, who was playing happily with a few Elves on the ground of the Rhakotis Library.

The faces of the Elves expressed sheer delight. They seldom had the opportunity to babysit humans. Rhodri basked in the attention from the Elves, who were almost his size. He communicated using gurgles and coos.

"We need to get a message out to Nicholas," Nest told Elissa as she scooped Rhodri in her arms. Standing upright to stretch, Nest affectionately kissed and rubbed her cheek against the top of his head. "The golden tara must be placed at Mount Kailash. We've got to grid it with Hill of Tara and Glastonbury Tor. Nicholas is our man."

"Great idea!" Elissa exclaimed. "How did you come up with Mount Kailash?"

"According to the documents, it is the mandala for the planet Earth," Nest replied.

"What will they think of next?" Elissa questioned. "I was just a glimmer in Dad's eyes when they came up with the mandala."

"Do you know the story?" Nest asked patted Rhodri, who had begun seeking her. She looked down at the hungry infant, "That's right, Mom on tap."

"It's another history lesson," Elissa said.

"Lay it on me, Mama," Nest said.

"It has to do with the Ring of Ascendance the Noris presented to the planet during creation," Elissa began. "A Noris woman named Indira wore the Ring of Ascendance. She fled Atlantis with the refugees led by Landon. After the destruction of the Northern Arctos, she journeyed to Mount Meru with a group from the Southern caves. The Serpentines destroyed the Arctos with lethal levels of electromagnetic radiation until the arterioles in their brains ruptured. Then they used powerful lasers on the mountains and caused them to collapse. This covered the evidence of the Serpentine attacks and experimentation. The Arctos's Dragon flyers from the southern Himalayan caves wanted to prevent another Serpentine attack. Indira provided cover for the Dragon flyers in Africa by throwing the ring into the volcano, which comprised Mount Meru. By this time, Indira had embodied the Ring of Ascendance. The volcano erupted as the life force of the planet accepted the ring. In a meditation, the lovers on Mount Kailash transported Indira's group through the ethers. They landed on Mount Kailash, which has four faces on it. Those meditating on Mount Kailash served as the yang connection to the yin volcano, collectively embodied as Shiva, also known as the enlightened transformer. The group that came from the volcano at Mount Meru became collectively known as Parvati. Attraction, or the dance of yin and yang, united the groups separated on the mountains, and saved the Shiva group."

Nest sat down to relax as Elissa paused. Rhodri began to close his eyes in contentment, drifting into a light sleep. She questioned Elissa, "So the Ring of Ascendance tilts the balance?"

"Those who comprise the Shiva connection can also transform the outcome, providing a more favorable solution." Elissa nodded. After accepting a cup of dragon grog from an Elf, the Sea Dragon queen resumed the history lesson.

"When the Brahmins fled Babylon after the Serpentines destroyed their tower, some of them joined the Celestial community at Mount Kailash. An alien spaceship caused the destruction of the Tower of Babylon, which initially was constructed as communication device. The tower helped the human family maintain contact with benevolent extraterrestrials. Kailash refers to the enlightened state achieved by some of the Brahmins, who had crystalized their pineal glands like the other inhabitants of the mountain. Pineal glands are sensitive to electromagnetic or radio frequencies. They are part of the mechanism for enlightened global communication. The enlightened Brahmins were given a new name, Vishnu, to denote their new status as preservers of the balance. Collectively, they comprised a threesome that could be gridded with the earth's Four Directions. Later, it was this Trinity that inspired Patrick and Alec the Green Knight during their travels to India."

Nest swallowed hard. She had heard the story of Alec the Green Knight, otherwise known to the Roman Britons as the Green Man. He had been crucified with two other knights near the Castle Marlboro. The Serpentines had intended to crucify all Green Knights, who particularly contained the earth's spirit.

Elissa watched Nest's face grow ashen. Nest moved her sleeping baby from her breast and placed him comfortably on a mat on the library floor. Then she stood and wiped a tear from her eye.

"The golden tara must go back to Mount Kailash by way of Mehrugarh," Nest said as she turned away. Tears came flooding down her cheeks as the young woman began sobbing uncontrollably. She had never made the connection between her ancestors and the Noris. Nest quickly left the room to purge her insides.

"I think that we need another human in the mix," an Elf commented. "Dragons, Elves, and infants don't cut it here."

At that moment, Kuan Yin appeared in one of the hallways that converged into the main room. Elissa looked up at the time traveler. The Elf shot a desperate look of panic at the goddess of compassion.

"I heard that the golden tara is being relocated," she said. "I gave it to Nest's ancestor several hundred years ago when she was a young mother. There something about raising a generation in the midst of chaos that move mothers to tears. It is poignant, but it is the edge that provides the advantage. It makes them not only unstoppable in their determination, but untouchable to most."

"That's the mission," Elissa responded. "We need a little balance here, first."

"What do you mean?" Kuan Yin asked her as she looked at the sleeping baby lying on a ground mat.

"Like Joslin, there's another new mother who has lost it," Elissa said. "Remember the time when you presented the golden tara to Joslin?"

"Yes, Joslin was Nest's great-grandmother. I think Joslin was crying over the future of Tinka, Nest's grandmother, as an infant. Apparently, I've arrived for another overwhelming postpartum moment," she observed. "When the past has been so violently despairing, these young mothers become upset when they consider the future of their babies. The tears mark a rite of passage, where they rise like a phoenix from the ashes to transcend the looming situation. They also collectively embody the Ring of Ascendance."

"This is more universal," Elissa agreed.

"Obviously. Tinka went on to establish the Kingdom of the Golden Tara as a result of her experiences. We have come full circle here." Then Kuan Yin asked, "Where is Nest?"

"Down the next corridor," Elissa replied.

Kuan Yin hurried down the corridor. She found Nest crying hysterically in an adjacent room. Sitting down next to Nest, Kuan Yin put her arm around her.

"Don't forget to grid the portals in Antarctica," she reminded the queen, warmly giving Nest a gentle rock with her extended arm.

"I know," Nest answered softly. "I'll figure it out."

"The other star seed civilizations came through portals in Antarctica," Kuan Yin continued as she pulled Nest closer.

"I heard," Nest gasped between tears.

"You have it in your blood, you know," Kuan Yin told her.

"The Green Knights, Jesse, and Arcas," Nest said. "I feel these issues very deeply."

"That's what makes you so strong," Kuan Yin persisted. "You are the first generation to get it."

"If I can get over the trauma of the past," she said as she dried her eyes.

"When you can, then we can," Kuan Yin told her. "It was bond of love that brought these souls through the portal. That's enough to move anyone to tears. The Serpentines don't understand this, which gives you the tactical advantage."

"If you say so," she blubbered.

"I say so. These souls came a long way to be united with each other again," Kuan Yin told her. "Do you think that they are going to give up now?"

"No," Nest honestly answered.

"What is so important about bringing the golden tara through Mehrugarth?" Kuan Yin asked her. "I overheard that part of the conversation."

Nest looked at Kuan Yin in the eye. "Other Atlantean survivors surfaced there. They are vulnerable and we must connect with them."

"How do you know?" asked Kuan Yin asked.

"I feel it in my blood," she confessed. "During the intergalactic wars, they immigrated to the Indus Valley."

Kuan Yin speculated, "You may be correct. We'll get Nicholas to take the golden tara to them and see what catches the light. The icon will filter the grid for spiritual predators, while serving as a beacon for those we may have lost to history."

Nest quieted and nodded. "The Lemurian insurgents landed there by watercraft. Only three Lemurian insurgents died destroying the crystal."

"It's the Druid blood," Kuan Yin surmised.

"I know," Nest said, rising from her position. "Though not all blood is thicker than water. This is called circulation, the life-giving ties that bond. I'm not referring to stasis."

"Stasis, hmm, are you politely referring to traitors in our midst?" Kuan Yin questioned, standing to confront Nest.

"There's more in the community besides Merfyn, Tristan, Coleus, and Eilene. Most promoted their own cause," Nest revealed.

"I see why it is a touchy subject," Kuan Yin said. "It is not me that you need. I sense that it is someone else."

"Mehrgarh served as the port of entry after the Serpentines destroyed Mu, the original star of the Leumurians," Nest reasoned. "They don't need a light filter like the others. They need our time. They have been living on borrowed time."

"That's an interesting concept," Kuan Yin told Nest. "They just need to be held to the planet."

"Yes, Nicholas can do it," Nest reflected. "He is complete within himself. Please go to him with my love. I presented him the golden tara shortly before I tied the knot with Elise. Have him take the golden tara to Mount Kailash by way of Mehrgarh. He'll understand the need to grid ascendance in the network. Nicholas is my partner in this, and I can track him in my meditations. It will be like I am there with him, except I am too exhausted to travel. Besides, I sense that he has a loose end to tie up with a past lover on Mount Kailash. The collective consciousness wants to avoid another disaster like what happened at the Glastonbury Tor, where the Serpentine Britons razed the abbey. We all must deepen our relationships to each other to solidify the bonds. If he ever makes it as pope, he'll need the connection with his yin counterpart from Glastonbury Tor. They both need to heal the past to strengthen the gridding with the Kingdom of Tara."

Kuan Yin promised that she would fill in for Nest, so that she could rest. The time traveler had stayed and comforted Nest until she regained her cheerfulness and stamina. She helped the Elves gather more information on the mission to Mount Kailash. Both she and Nest researched all the angles to address future concerns.

Chapter Thirteen

Two weeks later, Kuan Yin took an Elf with her to Patara. She appeared to Nicholas while he was cleaning up the sacristy. Looking up from his activity, he saw her standing in the doorway.

"Kuan Yin, what brings you here?" Nicholas asked, offering her a chair.

"We want you to take the golden tara to Mount Kailash by way of Mehrgarh," she told him.

"That's a great idea," he said as sat down next to her. "I was arriving at a similar conclusion here in the east. We need to incorporate the notion of ascendance in these troubled times."

"How do you know?" Kuan Yin asked, perplexed.

"It is not just mothers with newborns, who have been experiencing an overwhelming sense of hopelessness and futility. They are only the harbingers. At least they can release the emotion through tears. I see it in the eyes of the people in town," he replied. "They appear dead before they are old. A part of them is gone."

She pressed Nicholas. Noting his awareness, she asked him, "How did you managed to escape it?"

"I keep the light of the winter solstice in my heart," he told her. "It helps to have jolly ol' Saint Nikolaos as a mentor, even if he is a mutant merman."

Kuan Yin laughed. "I see. There is nothing better than reveling in the joy of the earth spirits to take one's mind off things. I can see how you achieved becoming the King of the Universe. You have managed to keep it all in perspective."

"It helps to be surrounded by Elves. They have collectively overcome similar heartaches in their own past." He grinned at Kuan Yin's traveling companion. "How are they getting along at the Rhakotis Library?"

"It's a marriage made in heaven between the child and childlike," she replied. "Rhodri and the Elves were meant for each other. They brighten up the place while keeping the excitement down to a dull roar."

"Wonderful. I knew Nest was on to something when she suggested it," he added. "Just as long as they don't become a major distraction."

"So far, so good," Kuan Yin observed. "Nest enjoys their cheerful company."

"Great, I am so happy to hear that she is doing so well with them. We need all the cheer we can get as we free ourselves from the bondage that existed long before earth was created. Some star systems were annihilated by the dark forces. Only soul fragments remain, and those who attacked them attached to these fragments like leeches. Now, about these souls that have been arriving on the planet either wounded or hunted by demons..." he began. "...I have something to offer. My idea is to get rid of the leeches before we recover the spirits. Otherwise, we are vulnerable."

"Please, tell me," Kuan Yin said.

"I can grid the starlight line from the black hole to Greenland with the Lemurian base at Mehrgarh," he proposed.

"How are you going to do that?" she asked.

"Water," he said simply.

"Water?" Kuan Yin questioned further. "How is that going to work?"

"Water brings heaven to earth in its reflection," he offered.

"You have point there," she agreed. "Go for it."

Then she faded into the surrounding atmosphere like an apparition. Nicholas remained still for a moment, reflecting on his next undertaking.

****

After packing quickly, he went to bed early to rest before his trip. The next morning, Nicholas left for Mehrgarh. Deciding to leave the Elves at home in Patara, he arrived in Mehrgarh with nothing more than the golden tara and a flying reindeer. He did not have the slightest notion what he was going to do in Mehrgarh. Rather than waste more time deliberating his next move, he slapped the reindeer on the hindquarters and told him to go forage. Then he walked straight for the underground tombs in the center of town.

"Hey man, where did you get the red fur parka, tuque, and boots?" a hawker on the street asked him. "What an upbeat fashion statement!"

"Patara," Nicholas replied. "We incorporate the spirit of Christmas in our style, or maybe vice-versa. It doesn't matter. We find occasion to enjoy ourselves regardless of the weather and terrain."

"Would you like to trade?" he asked. "How about a turban for the tuque?"

"Sure," Nicholas answered, swapping his hat for the turban. He continued making his way through town.

"Don't you look good! You must be new in town," a princess, who happened to be riding on the street in a caravan, shouted at him. She hopped off the platform and stopped Nicholas. Her fingers lightly ran over the buttons on his fur parka. Then she stood back a few steps and examined him.

Wondering why he had ever volunteered for this mission, Nicholas maintained his own counsel, and remained silent underneath the scrutiny. He sighed, conveying his impatience with her hint of familiarity. Like the other encounter in Patara, he was being welcomed as a curiosity rather than a man.

"Aren't you hot?" she asked.

"Only in bed," he told her with a naive shrug. He preferred bringing the interaction down to his level. Focused on his mission, Nicholas wasn't interested in superficial conversations about appearances. After having traveled this far to get to Patara, he could care less what the inhabitants thought of him. Wishing to get straight to business, he silently vowed to not linger in any one particular place. Under the circumstances, Nicholas chose to ignore his discomfort in being out of his element.

"Aren't you jolly? Is that a proposition?" she questioned, not seeming the least bit intimidated by the man in the red parka. She felt that she had seen him somewhere before. Realizing that he was a deja vu, she pressed him further and stepped closer to man in the red parka like a bee to honey.

"No, it's the truth," he replied. "I am in over my head here. I'm not wearing anything else underneath, and I am feeling self-conscious in this part of the world. This attire is my custom."

"Great. Now I understand the reason for the attraction. Well, I have another truth for you," she said. "I foresaw your arrival in a meditation I had this morning. My job is to escort you to a spring in the town garden."

"Let's go. You're the best sense of direction that I've had in a long time," Nicholas told the princess. Then he added after a moment to reflect, "Honestly."

"I had that feeling about you. You seemed lost. It is as if you need me," she retorted. "Climb aboard and sit beside me, before you lose the shirt off your back. By the way, do you happen to have a golden tara on you?"

He produced the golden tara from his pocket. Nicholas proudly showed it to her. He knew how to make her happy. When she nodded in satisfaction, he joined her on the draped pavilion. The footmen carrying the pavilion headed toward the town spring.

"Wash the golden tara in the spring," she instructed when they arrived at the site. "I understand that it has been through a lot lately. It needs to be refreshed before you continue your journey."

Nicholas did as she said. He began the rinsing the icon in the cool waters of the spring. The water bubbled down a small green ditch and washed over the icon. Suddenly, he stopped and took a deep breath.

"What do you feel?" she asked him as she knelt beside him.

"It's a memory," he responded, submerging the golden tara further in the rushing waters.

"What is it telling you?" she asked him.

"It is a long forgotten one, over two million years old," he stated. Removing the golden tara from the water, he sat down to fathom his experience. "Now I know why I was compelled to journey to Mehrgarh." After a moment's pause, he wiped a tear from his eye with the admission. "I needed to get in touch with a major aspect of myself."

"Don't cry about it," she instructed. "I am not going to support you."

"I won't cry," he said resolutely. "I've quit fighting it."

"What is here?" she continued to guide him.

"A life," he said, staring off into space.

"Keep going. You are being rather cryptic," the princess commented. "I think that you are on to something."

"I know," Nicholas confessed. "I've always been a man of few words."

"Speak up now," she said. "Here is your chance. Now or never."

"OK," he told her as he rose with the golden tara tucked underneath his arm. "I have found a secure sense of permanence here, unlike anywhere else on the planet. We are staying with the earth."

"Excellent," the princess encouraged him. "I knew that you would agree with me once you touched the water."

"Why?" he asked slowly. "Why does this spot hold such an answer?"

"It's history," she said. "This was the very first Celestial settlement on the planet. The tears that they cried were ones of joy rather than sorrow. Emotion is embedded in the place."

"The Lemurians were the very first Celestial refugees here," he asserted. "They arrived intact, whereas the other Celestials were wounded. They came through portals in Greenland and Antarctica."

"Well done. Now, take the golden tara to Mount Kailash," she advised him. "Tell them that it truly comes from a place of joy."

Nicholas kissed her lightly on the forehead. Smiling at the princess, he asked, "Mount Kailash is the mandala for the planet. How did that happen?"

"When the refugees from the Centaurus Galaxy entered the black hole as soul fragments, they arrived in portals on Greenland," she began. "There was one exception: this soul carried the Ring of Ascendance. Due to heavy persecution by the Serpentine Federation, the soul missed the black hole. The soul was caught by a Celestial on Arcturus. Somehow, the Arcturian attracted this wounded soul. The soul carrying the Ring of Ascendance had gone to the fifth dimension to escape. The fifth dimension pertains to the rotational moment of time. The Arcturian was named Gus. After having helped create the Ring of Determination, he fell in love with the soul bearing the Ring of Ascendance. He gave the Ring of Determination to one of his Arcturian friends to bring through the portal, while he carried the ring bearer from the Centaurus Galaxy. After the souls adopted the human form, the ring bearer went to Mount Kailash on a platform with other Noris. Gus met up with his buddies in Mehrgarh."

"Happy Solstice!" Nicholas said changing the subject abruptly as he prepared to leave for Mount Kailash. He felt too overwhelmed with emotion to pursue his studies with the princess any further.

"Thank you for sharing your celebration with us!" the princess called, watching Nicholas hurry out of the garden in search of his flying reindeer.

Chapter Fourteen

Nicholas journeyed to the top of Mount Kailash with the golden tara safely cushioned inside a pocket of his parka. Preferring to summit the mountain on foot, he left his flying reindeer at the base of the mountain. A half-mile from the top, Nicholas stopped at a small town where several people rushed out of their mountain huts to meet him. Inviting him in their homes, they gave him broth and flat bread. Between meals, he traded his boots for suitable hiking shoes to traverse the cold, rugged terrain. Leaving the villagers early the next morning, Nicholas resumed his trek with a quick smile and wave.

As he eyed the trail before him, it occurred to him that maybe he never should have stopped for refreshments. Realizing that he was procrastinating in facing the inevitable, he sought encouragement from the traders. Nicholas didn't fear climbing the mountain, it was the woman sitting on top of it. He had known the high priestess in his youth. At the time, she wasn't a high priestess on Mount Kailash. She was Druid priestess hiding in the Glastonbury abbey as a nun. When the Serpentine Britons realized what was going on in their town, they razed the place and the inhabitants with it. Some survived and escape, terribly marred by the experience.

"You are almost there. The terrain becomes more treacherous as you get to your destination. We expect a blizzard on the summit within the next few hours. You don't have much time to ascend," one told him. "Follow the prayer flag line, otherwise you will go over the edge."

After taking a deep breath, Nicholas nodded his thanks and hurried before the next snowstorm came. Carefully finding his footing on every step, he silently expressed gratitude for his nickname, Lucky. The terrain succeeded in altering his consciousness. He no longer felt as if he existed on the planet. Reaching the heavy wooden doors of the lodge near the peak, he entered without knocking. He walked through a dimly lit hallway past several motionless, masked guards. A strong light emerged from a distant room at the end of the hall. A young priestess silently meditated at the far end of the room. Two large black pumas sat beside on her on one end. They awoke and stood when he approached her.

"Been hitting the opium hard lately?" he asked her.

She smiled softly before opening her eyes to address his remarks. "We are a changing world," she answered. "What once grounded us now has become an overindulgence. We quit the stuff here years ago."

"We must be making progress," he responded, sitting down on the bare wooden floor in front of her. Nicholas crossed his feet over his legs and assumed a similar meditative position.

"Kuan Yin and the Princess of Mehrgarh let me know that you were coming." The woman observed, "I understand that you have a way with women."

"Many," he warned her. "I have a past with a Druid priestess. Now I am in a partnership with a Celtic princess. I am a very lucky."

The black pumas separated and resumed their sitting position, surrounding the woman like two bookends. She laughed quietly at his last remark. Snapping her fingers, the priestess summoned the silent guards lining the hallway. They entered the room and lifted Nicholas to his feet, hauling him away as the pumas followed and watched. Without injuring him, they pushed him inside a room several doors down the hall. Guards confiscated his shoes and hat before leaving him alone in the cell.

"Cool your heels," one advised him before slamming the door shut behind them.

Nicholas sat down on the small bed and covered his head with his hands in anguish. A bitter memory pierced his soul and he slowly began to cry. He could remember her being pursued by a band of Serpentine Romans during an attack on Glastonbury Tor. Nicholas recalled being beaten until he could no longer see where she had fled. When he had composed himself, he reclined on the bed and examined the contents of the room. The cell was simply furnished. Staring at the ceiling, he created images from the random designs of the woodwork. His thoughts were interrupted by the sudden arrival of the priestess. The woman entered the room from a hidden door in the wall. She was clad in nothing more than a white veil. The two black pumas emerged behind her and quickly positioned themselves beside her. The beasts growled at Nicholas until he acknowledged the appearance of the woman. They left only a small space for his approach.

Nicholas immediately rose from the bed and stood close to her. The presence of the pumas in the room left him with no choice. He faced her. For a brief moment he deliberated whether to embrace her or remove his parka.

"Remove your parka. I want the golden tara," she told him. "You can keep the tears."

"You drive a hard bargain," he said. Then he fibbed for the sake of irony, "I haven't seen you in a while." He referred to the distant past, rather than the present. It marked the life that they had once shared. Instead of removing his parka, he ripped off her veil. Holding her nude body in his arms he kissed her deeply until she succumbed to his pressure. The cats in the room purred loudly as he placed her down on the bare wood floor. Standing over her, he hurriedly unbuttoned his parka and yielded the golden tara. She languidly opened her eyes and saw him holding the golden tara over her. Stooping over her collapsed figure, he placed the icon above her head and entered her. She squirmed as she felt him again. It had been a long time since their lives together in Glastonbury.

"What goes on at Mount Kailash, stays inside Mount Kailash. I want to keep the parka too," she whispered in his ear as her moist tongue ran circles along his ear lobe.

Delirious from the moistness of her body, he again plunged into her. When she screamed, he knew that he had captured her with his soul. A light bite on the lobe of his ear drew blood, but he remained stoically silent, past the point of words.

"You'll make a great a pope," she gasped underneath his quiet weight. "Don't forget us, the little people."

"How could I?" he uttered hoarsely as he rolled to her side. Covering her with his parka, he added, "You look great in red."

"I'll remember that," she said. Taking a deep breath, the temple priestess added, "For your next pilgrimage."

"You should have recovered by then." He told her, "For another round."

"Later," she admitted. "You can get too much of a good thing in this rarified atmosphere."

Lingering on the floor, she slowly lifted one arm and snapped her fingers. Several guards entered the space, bringing Nicholas a change of clothes and hiking boots for his trip down the mountain. He quickly put on the attire and leaned over the woman to kiss her goodbye. "How was it that we separated the last time?" he asked, shaking his head sorrowfully.

"Duress," she recalled, slightly rolling her eyes. Then she lied, knowing his last point of departure, "I think that it was in Turkey."

"Forget it and remember this," he urged, kissing her one more time. He raised his head with the comment, and saw the pain behind her intentional denial. She had placed herself with him in the present by mentioning Turkey. Nicholas played her game and commented, "The soldiers are well trained. They seem to read your mind."

"We have learned to read each other's minds," she softly said. "At the top of the world, you are left with nothing except your thoughts."

"Nothing," he agreed, peering underneath his jacket one more time. "Nothing." Then he ran his hand smoothly over the contour of her body. Ending with several gentle, reassuring strokes. He encouraged her, "Stay warm."

Nodding slightly, she turned her face away and drifted into a deep sleep. Standing upright, he snapped his fingers. Several ninjas came in the room and picked up her limp form without protest.

"Take her to bed. Make sure that she stays comfortable," he commanded. Then he left the cell behind them.

He watched them carry her down the hall as he headed for the same door that he entered. Stepping outside the lodge, he felt the blast of cold mountain air hit his face. Nicholas's ear stung with pain and he reached to staunch the drop of his own blood between his fingers. His lover had left her mark, while he had only left her a red parka and golden icon. After licking the red ooze from his hand, he began his journey down the mountain.

The trek took half as much time as the climb. Nicholas's ride stood waiting for him at the base of the mountainous terrain. Mounting his flying reindeer, he turned for one last look at the four-faced mountain. Several overhead clouds veiled it from view to anyone further below him on the terrain. Nicholas squeezed the reindeer between his legs and they flew back to Turkey.

He flew high in the sky. Landing near the abandoned village of Patara, he searched for a suitable place to hide the reindeer from returning inhabitants. He knew that the town would soon be populated once the locals sensed the positive shift in collective consciousness. After leaving the flying reindeer in a forest near the church, he hurried to the sacristy for a change into his priestly clothes. Kuan Yin met him in the small room as he finished buttoning his cassock. He looked up at her.

"News travels fast," she said. "You've entered the circle."

"I still feel it in my head," he remarked.

"It is a mandala of consciousness for the world," she told him.

"For the world we know," he added.

"As we *know* it," she said dreamily. "Thank you."

Then she faded from his view like Mount Kailash behind the veil of white clouds. He looked down at the floor and then hurried to the window. Snowflakes fell over the town in a white haze. He pulled back from the window as a memory stirred his emotions. Remembering the mists surrounding the Tor at Glastonbury, his lips savored the woman that he had just left on the mountain. Suddenly, he knew that he would always be able to find her behind the veil, somewhere beneath the shadows of his soul.

"Happy Solstice," he said out loud, realizing that Kuan Yin would be able to hear him.

Peering out the window again, he noticed a light gust of wind swirl snowflakes in circle. He smiled to himself, realizing that his prayers had been heard. His ring got caught on the fabric of his sleeve. The metal softly ripped the skin, leaving a delicate bloody scratch across his middle finger. He brought it his mouth and tasted the blood. It was his.

Chapter Fifteen

Several months later, Nicholas traveled through a series of portals to the Rhakotis Library where he met Nest, who was researching another topic.

"How's little Rhodri?" Nicholas asked, scooping the baby in his arms.

Nest rose from the piles of papyrus around her and kissed Nicholas lightly on the cheek. She whispered softly into his healed ear, "I hear that it went well at Mount Kailash."

Grinning a little, Nicholas answered truthfully, "Very well. Some things don't change."

"Weren't you two a couple at Glastonbury?" Nest asked as she took Rhodri from him.

"Once upon a time." He sighed. "Long story." He quickly changed the subject. "What are we going to do about Petra, Jordan?"

"I am planning to visit Jordan," Nest answered nonchalantly.

"How did Elissa and her beau ever managed to pull it off in a Blue's base?" he asked.

"She wants toddlers," Nest quipped. "Elissa timed it with Rhodri's ability to walk."

"She wandered into a Blue's base!" he protested.

"I think that she wants us to retake it," Nest reasoned.

"It is the only way to hatch those Dragon eggs," he agreed. "How is Curtis is able to watch the eggs without being detected?"

"I don't know. We should ask Elissa," Nest surmised. "I think that she's getting her nails polished in the Dragon stall."

"Let's go talk to her," he urged Nest. "Young Rhodri will be toddling soon."

They ventured to the end of the next hall where Elissa was being groomed.

"Hi, Nicholas," Elissa said as her caretaker buffed her nails. "I hear that it went well at Mount Kailash."

"Good news travels fast," he said with a low whistle. Wisely, he directed the conversation back to immediate business. "How is it that Curtis is able to watch the Dragon eggs without being detected?"

"The Blues are convinced that he belongs to them," she answered.

"Do they know about the Dragon eggs?" Nest asked.

"No, they think that Curtis is just a poor, lost Sea Dragon," Elissa told them.

"Are they stupid?" Nicholas questioned.

"Yes," Nest replied nonchalantly. Turning to face Nicholas, she proposed, "Elise and I will retake Petra. Do you mind babysitting Rhodri? He really enjoys the Elves."

"It's a deal," he declared. "It will help satisfy my paternal yearnings for the moment."

"It will give you both some time to bond before he replaces Merfyn as King and you become Pope."

"I smell success," Nicholas said as he lifted the child to him. He told Nest, "First, you must show me how to change a diaper."

"No problem," she said. "I need a break from the library."

"How did we lose Petra?" he asked as they walked.

"During the intergalactic wars, it was Furry Dragon base," Nest explained. "All the buildings were made big enough to fit dragons."

"How did the Blues take it?" Nicholas questioned.

"Infiltration," she replied. "The story is here on this sheet of papyrus. They used a form of mind-control and reprogrammed the Dragon flyers."

"That's deadly," he said, cuddling Rhodri.

"Yes, the Blues got inside the heads of the Furry Dragons," she said. "They all went on suicide missions."

"How do we protect ourselves?" he asked.

"Good question," she replied. "I haven't figured that one out yet."

Nicholas thought for a moment, then he began chuckling. "I don't think that you need to worry. Elissa pulled a calculated, shrewd move when she nested at Petra. She is moving you to great achievements."

"Do you mind cluing me in?" she asked Nicholas.

"It is obvious to me that you have the instinctual nature of a mama bear making the world safe for her wandering bear cub. Even if Elissa put you up to it, your maternal overdrive makes you unstoppable."

"You have a point," Nest replied as she took Rhodri from Nicholas again. She lightly tickled his Buddha belly and playfully tossed him around. A laugh erupted from the great depths of the infant as he gazed into his mother's eyes. Nest smiled at Rhodri's hearty, youthful laughter. She cooed at him. "You really would like to play with some baby Sea Dragons, wouldn't you little Rhodri?"

The baby clapped his hands together and happily murmured, "Mama, mama, mama."

"I rest my case," Nicholas commented. "When do you leave for Petra?"

"Tomorrow, after Elise arrives," Nest told him while continuing to mouth a conversation with Rhodri. "I want to strike while I am hot."

****

The next day, Elissa, Elise, and Nest traveled through a series of portals to Petra. They emerged in a large dark room where Elissa had left her eggs. They saw Curtis lying in the far corner. His shiny liquid silver scales shone eerily in the moonlight. He was curled around several shiny objects. Nobody was in sight.

"Where is everybody?' Nest asked.

"Curtis scared them," Elissa mentioned. "They thought that he was the ghost of the Dragons they killed."

"I thought you said that they had taken him in as forlorn, lost dragon," Nest reminded her.

"I lied," Elissa said. "Sort of."

"What? I trusted you!" Nest insisted. "If you can't trust your Sea Dragon, who can you trust?"

Suddenly, there was a loud noise at the entrance to the room.

"Who goes there?" an alien dressed in a blue astronaut suit yelled.

He immediately began firing his laser gun blindly in the room. The volley of fire awoke Curtis, who merely lifted his sleepy fatherly head and reflected the rays back with his liquid scales. Nest turned and hurled her sword at the rushing attack in the room.

"Lied again," Elissa said, ducking to avoid the reflected laser volley.

"Now I am really mad!" Nest shouted as she destroyed the onslaught. "This really ticks me off. First, my Dragon lies to me, and now we have these Blues stealing my eggs. Elissa, get a move on it and throw me a flame. You owe me big time, girl."

"Righty-o." The golden Sea Dragon queen complied, tossing a flame Nest's way.

Nest caught the flame with the top of her ormuz sword. It became a torch, which she used to ignite the line of blue astronauts streaming toward her. Immediately, the spacesuits caught fire and quickly spread through the ranks. A line of fire snaked its way through Petra until it struck the Blue's spaceships. They all exploded.

Satisfied that the damage had been done, Nest left Elissa to clean up the mess. She hurried over to Elise, who had been using the sleepy paternal dragon as both a shield and a weapon. Skillful placement of the limp tail and limbs of the dragon reflected the laser fire back to the Blues. Overwhelmed by emotion, Nest flung her arms around Elise when he rose from behind Curtis. The couple passionately kissed and hugged each other as Elissa went to town. Curtis continued to doze. Elise calmed his partner and pointed to some shiny objects underneath Curtis.

"They look just like their father, except they are as hard as diamonds!" he exclaimed. Kneeling beside the Sea Dragon eggs, he knocked on the shells. "They *are* diamonds, but I've never seen diamonds of these colors—green, orange, brown, red, blue, and purple."

"Hmm," Nest said, standing back from the nest. "I dreamt about these eggs. How many are there?"

"There's another room full of eggs behind these," Elise said. "There could be thousands."

"Seventeen thousand to be exact," Elissa announced. She wiped her hands on each other to erase the effects of her last dirty job.

"No wonder Curtis is so tired," Elise said.

"You lied to me," Nest accused her Sea Dragon.

"Not really," Elissa said. "Remember your dream? I fed it to you."

"Huh?" Nest asked, perplexed and confused.

"Back in the olden days, Sea Dragons used dreams to communicate to their flyers and caretakers before meeting them. It is how we called them. Dreams are the best defense against mind-control or programming. Dreams are messages from the soul."

"That is irrelevant!" Nest responded with a touch of anger in her voice. "Don't do it again."

"What?" Elissa questioned.

"Don't lie to me again," Nest demanded. "The end doesn't justify the means."

"Maybe it does," the golden Sea Dragon queen replied. "I wasn't the first to emotionally manipulate you. Take Rhodri, for example."

"They start off young, don't they?" Nest posed rhetorically. "Don't do it again!"

"You won back a base that had been in enemy hands for over a thousand years. What more do you want?" Elissa asked.

"Truth," Nest replied.

"You are being tempered," Elissa said. "That is the truth. Now you know what you are capable of."

"Tempered for what?" she asked.

"Twins," the Sea Dragon queen announced.

"Hmm, I had a dream about that too," Nest murmured in temporary resignation.

Chapter Sixteen

"Don't worry, Nest will get over it when she sees the babies," Elise promised the Sea Dragon queen.

Elissa remained with Curtis while Nest returned to Winchcombe Abbey and soon learned that she was pregnant. Nine months later, Nest forgave Elissa.

"Don't do it again," she reminded the Sea Dragon queen, who had come to Winchcombe Abbey to see the twins.

The dark-haired girl was named Angharad and the light-haired one was called Esyllt. Knowing that Rhodri would succeed Merfyn's throne, the light-haired twin had been given the name of Merfyn's courier, who was known also known as Morgasia. This would help deceive the Serpentine Britons and Romans when the twins matured in the legal world. Both girls had fallen asleep at the same time for a brief moment and Nest rested on the bed as she spoke to Elissa. She had delivered at Winchombe Abbey to be close to Elise. "I need all the help that I can get with these two girls. They act like yin and yang. When one is asleep, the other is awake. They never seem to get together on a project."

"How about if I take Rhodri out to see the Sea Dragon eggs at Petra?" Elissa offered. "He could use a break from his sisters, who keep everyone up all the time."

"He does seemed be overwhelmed by the double trouble," Nest agreed as she resumed nursing one infant while the other slept. "He could use a change of scenery."

"Yes, and he toddles very well now. Doesn't talk as much as Gerwyn did, but his nonverbal skills are fantastic," Elissa added.

"Rhodri!" Nest called from her reclined position on the bed.

Rhodri appeared from his position under the bed. He had been tracking the movements of cat, who had led him on a wild chase around the room. He handed his mother the cat toy that he had found during his pursuit.

"Thanks, Rhodri," Nest told him as she accepted the slimy cat toy from his chubby fingers. "Rhodri, how would you like to go with Elissa to see some Sea Dragon eggs?"

"For me!" he said rubbing his hands together in delight.

Nest smiled at him, before glancing at Elissa. "He's ready. He knows the word *mine*."

"Let's go pack, Rhodri," Elissa instructed as ushered the toddler out of the room before one of his sisters screamed.

"Bye, Mom." He proudly smiled as he followed Elissa out the door.

****

Though she was busy nursing the new babies, Nest still felt concern for her wandering son. She knew better than to stop him, the least that she could do was teach him how to slow down and remember to be safe. Nest waited patiently for her intrepid son to return from his adventure. The next day, Rhodri returned with seventeen Sea Dragon eggs. He delightedly pulled them out of Elissa's pouch, showing his mother each egg, one by one.

"Mine," he said when he deposited the first one on the floor below her feet. Then he hurried to Elissa's pouch for the next egg. Elissa quietly watched him with an expression of sheer maternal joy on her face.

"Put them in the corner over there, dear," Nest directed him. Then she spoke to Elissa in hushed voice, "*Seventeen eggs?* You are spoiling him worse than his Grandmother Patty."

"He was so determined." Elissa sighed. "He knew exactly which ones were his."

"*His?*" Nest exclaimed.

"*Mine*," Elissa repeated.

One of the babies began fussing with Nest's agitation.

"Shh," Elissa said as she helped Rhodri fish another egg from her pouch. "It's a long story."

"Let's have it," Nest demanded. "I'm not going anywhere soon. I have plenty of time here with nursing twins."

"He needs them," Elissa started.

88

"What is Rhodri going to do with seventeen eggs?" she asked Elissa.

"Divide the Three Collas," Elissa replied.

"One Colla is easier to deal with than three. Sounds like a plan," Nest thoughtfully considered, cocking her head side to side. "I can just imagine the possibilities."

"Instead of one Dragon base, we'll set up four. They will all be energetically connected like spokes on a wheel," Elissa continued.

"I like that," Nest said. "Nicholas and I have been gridding planetary mandalas," she said. "It would be powerful to set up Rhodri that way. I am all for feeling centered these days. Let me guess, the center will be the Hill of Tara, the heart of the Kingdom of the Golden Tara."

"You've got it," Elissa responded. "When the time comes, Rhodri's mandala will slip into another dimension for another thousand years."

"That should shake things up," Nest decided. "We must get it in place before the Grays inspire another Viking invasion."

"They have their sights on Northern France," Elissa said. "I think they want to intermarry with Carolus's brood."

"They should have fun with that," Nest commented facetiously. "Meanwhile, we'll set things up for Merlin's descendants. He was the only wizard that survived the Eye in the Sky. Great-grandmother Joslin helped him rebirth, otherwise he would have lost his mind like the other mutant mermen. Those who chose to become wizards were Merwyns, and they all drowned once they forgot that they were not fish anymore."

"The Viking Normans from France and the Noris from Scandinavia are two different factions," Elissa remarked, changing the focus of discussion.

"One partnered with the Priory of Scion while the other was called to Tara by the Stone of Destiny," Nest recounted.

"The ones settling into Normandy don't know that," Elissa said.

"The lineage determined by the Stone of Destiny never makes it into their Latin paperwork," Nest retorted.

"That's why the Stone of Destiny summoned Merlin's progeny to the Hill of Tara," Elissa speculated. "Only the locals will know the difference."

"The result is history and we know what that means. It's the reason the Dragon flyers have their own archivists," Nest continued. Then she turned her head toward Rhodri, who was busy rearranging his Sea Dragon in the corner. "When do the eggs hatch?"

"After Merfyn leaves the Hill of Tara," Elissa replied.

"When will that be?" Nest asked.

"Oh, you didn't hear," Elissa said. "Your spouse on paper was sent by Morgasia to destroy Aed Collas Menn. He left the Hill of Tara months ago."

"Doesn't he know the prophecy?" Nest asked. "Whoever kills a Collas will never be High King of Ireland."

"He was too busy spending time with Morgasia in England," Elissa commented. "Only Aquitaine recognizes Merfyn as King of Ulaid, which means that he must defend Eamhain Mhacha against the invading Collas. If he refuses, then the leadership in Aquitaine will realize that he is an imposter."

"Hmm, I am too busy with the twins to become involved with politics. Their arrival provided protection by keeping me out of the fray," Nest remarked as she removed a sleeping infant from her breast before the other one awoke. "They will probably burn Eamhain Mhacha. There goes the site for our wedding anniversary."

"It has already been abandoned and placed in a multidimensional portal," Elissa told her. "It won't be the same, but everyone knows how to access it."

"All I have to do is take care of the universe, everyone one else takes care of Ireland, Scotland, and Wales," Nest observed. "Thank you for looking after me."

"All of us have a role," Elissa acknowledged. "We keep each other safe. Now would you rub my back scales?"

A knock on the door of their suite interrupted them. A young monk entered the room. He smiled as he glanced at the young family of twins, toddler, and dragon.

"Merfyn killed Aed Collas Menn," he told them. "Now he has incurred the wrath of the Kingdom of Airghialla. We give him no more than two years to live."

"Wonderful! Now is it Elise's moment to befriend Airghialla," Nest observed. "We can help them find Merfyn."

"Time to hatch those eggs," Elissa announced, joining Rhodri in the corner of the room.

Chapter Seventeen

Two years later, the descendants of the Collas Brothers killed Merfyn and his rule ended. The transference of power was simply a matter of empty paperwork with Rhodri inheriting the kingdom. Nobody mentioned that he was only three years old and nobody really cared. Nest continued being the power behind the throne, while four-year-old Rhodri played with his seventeen dragons. Like the shells from which they hatched, this crop of Sea Dragons sported a coat of thick, colored diamond scales.

"I think that it is time to share some of the new Sea Dragons with the other kingdoms," Nest told him one day. "How many do you want to take to the Glastonbury Tor?"

"Six," Rhodri confidently told her.

"All right. Put those Sea Dragons in a group over there," she instructed. "Now how many do you want to leave with Gilderoy's rebellion in Scotland?"

"Gilderoy gets...five Sea Dragons," he replied as he sorted the group.

"And the Hill of Tara?" she asked

"Three Sea Dragons go to the Hill of Tara," he announced, looking up at his mother.

"OK. Those can go over to that section," she told him. "That covers England, Scotland, and Ireland. Now how many Sea Dragons are left for Pembroke, Wales?"

"Three," he answered after counting the remaining Sea Dragons.

"Look, Rhodri, the new Sea Dragons came colored-coded for the region," his mother coached him. "All the Sea Dragons bound for Ireland have green diamond scales. The ones for England are orange, whereas the Welsh Sea Dragons have amber-colored diamonds."

"The Scottish Sea Dragons have a red diamond coat," Rhodri piped.

No sooner than he had finished his sentence, the door burst open and Rhodri's twin sisters raced in the room. One attempted to scoop several red Sea Dragons in her arms, while the other sister tackled Rhodri to the floor. The baby Sea Dragons fled and scattered in various directions.

"Mom, they are messing up my groups!" Rhodri yelled.

"Girls, leave the dragons and your older brother alone," Nest reprimanded.

"Puppy pile!" the twin shouted to her sister with the red diamond Sea Dragons.

The other sister immediately dropped the red diamond Sea Dragons and landed on Rhodri.

"Mom!" Rhodri cried as he wrestled his sisters.

"I'll take the head," the dark-haired child said to her light-haired sister. "You take the feet."

"I want the head. You take the feet," the light-haired twin insisted.

"Girls," Nest intervened as she sorted the pile of small wriggling bodies. She pulled Rhodri out and placed him upright on his feet. Meanwhile, his sisters began skirmishing with each other. She led Rhodri and his diamond Sea Dragon groups out of the room.

"How about you and Elissa take the Sea Dragons to their new homes?" she suggested. "I'll stay and teach your younger sisters better manners."

Rhodri called to his assortment of seventeen Sea Dragons. "C'mon guys, let's go on tour."

Rhodri and his merry band of Sea Dragons headed down the hall and out the door. Nest closed the door to the room where the sisters jousted and went to find her husband. Elise was resting in a large chair by a fire in another room.

"Rhodri is ready to go on a trip with his seventeen Sea Dragons," Nest told him, pulling up a chair from the fire. She took his hand as she sat beside him and they gazed at the embers together. Nest appreciated the quiet time.

"What are the twins doing?" he slowly asked.

"Wrestling in the other room," she replied. "I'll check in when I hear screams."

"I need to visit Wessex now that Alfie has passed on," Elise told her.

"I'll do it," Nest offered. "My face is not as familiar. I can catch up with Rhodri in Scotland afterward."

"I'll keep on eye on the twins," Elise promised.

Chapter Seventeen

****

Leaving the next day, Nest took a portal to Wessex and met with the progeny of Gerwyn, Grandmother Tinka's older brother, at Glastonbury Abbey. After the attack on Glastonbury Tor, Gerwyn's lover had fled to a secluded cave near Wessex, where she gave birth to twins. The twin boy and girl were raised in secret. Gerwyn did not learn about his children until many years later, long after he had married Fergie of Scotland.

"How is it going, Nest?" Alfred, the male twin, asked. "We heard that you have twin girls."

"Yes, they are a handful," she acknowledged. "I understand that you have taken to guerilla warfare now that Tinka has ascended."

"Yes, Aquitaine has a foothold here in the monasteries," Osberga, his twin sister added. "They took over Alfie's kingdom and gave it to a Henri. His name is Edward the Elder. They are sorcerers with the empire. Their base is at Utrecht in the Netherlands."

"That is where the tribe of Joseph emigrated after the intergalactic wars of ancient Egypt," Nest commented. "They called themselves Frisians."

"Wilibrord, the protégé of Aquitaine, drove them out of the region. They fled to Wales," Osberga added. "The Frisians settled at Barclodiad y Gawres on the Island of Brave Folk, Ynys y Cedairn."

"Well, that's in our Kingdom of Gwynedd," Nest observed. "Are they in league with the black Fairies there?'

"Yes," Alfred responded. "When the black Fairies left the Congo, they went to several islands in the United Kingdom. The Island of Brave Folk is one of the refugee sites and serves as a base of operations for the Frisians, who war with the Franks for the Netherlands. The Frisians have an alliance with the black Fairies."

"Whatever happened to the Sea Dragon base on the Congo?" Nest asked them.

"The Serpentine Britons forced it to go underground," Osberga answered. "You'll have to look very hard to find it, though the black Fairies could help you."

"Hmm," Nest thought out loud. "Where do I go next?"

"You must grid Rhodri's mandala tighter," Alfred replied. "Incorporate these other sites. Start with Jesse's grandchild, Cuscraid. He has been waiting to see you. Cuscraid was one of Crierwy's lovers. She is returning soon to help him ascend."

"Whew!" Nest exclaimed. "There isn't much time."

"No, the Priory of Scion intends to wipe out all of Jesse's descendants and substitute their own offspring," Alfred told her. Jesse had two sons with his life partner, Findchoem. His oldest son, Conchobar, protected Queen Mab when the Serpentines pursued the Fairy Kingdom. The Serpentines have an agenda to destroy all earth spirits, which includes Fairies and Merpeople."

"Jesse's other son, Amergin, became a poet," Osberga noted. "Conchobar's life partner was Dierdre, Patrick's granddaughter."

"Jesse's children remained on the earth plane for a long time," Alfred observed. "They were the grandchildren of the Lady of the Lake, a mermaid."

"It helps to be able to swim," Nest speculated. "Even if the waters are troubled."

"You are becoming a young philosopher." Osberga smiled.

Nest laughed. "It comes with the twins." Then she asked, "Where can I find Cuscraid these days?"

"Rath Lugh," Osberga answered. "He has been gridding the Ark of the Covenant with Rhodri's mandala."

"Oh, I am so glad people are taking the initiative," Nest said. "I'll go visit Cuscraid and tie him in the mandala. When Crierwy returns, she can grid the mandala behind the veil."

"That should bring everyone peace of mind," Osberga reflected.

"We will need it," Nest said.

Chapter Eighteen

"I'm so happy you came," Cuscraid greeted as he opened the door of his cottage. "You must be Creirwy's successor. She is so proud of you."

He invited her inside and offered her a chair by the hearth. Nest noticed that he appeared youthful and vibrant. Though she had never met Cuscraid, it was not difficult to imagine how the handsome man seduced her great-aunt Creirwy years ago. Now that he was almost two hundred and twenty-five years old, he was looking forward to meeting one of his former lovers in the next realm.

"I see Crierwy's ring on your hand. Did you bring her sword with you?" he asked, moving closer to her by the fire.

Nest took a deep breath and extended her hand to him. She could understand how this man had won the desire of her aunt. He softly kissed the ring and withdrew. Nest could feel his warm breath on her hand and lightly dropped it to her side. Feeling dazed by his gentle abruptness, she reached for Creirwy's sword in her travel bag without taking her eyes off him.

"The Lion sleeps tonight," she murmured.

Cuscraid chuckled softly at her words. He took the sword from her hand and examined it closely. Then he told her with a shooting glance, "It is a double-edged sword. We sleep while the Priory at Aquitaine sleeps."

"Let's not wake the Lion," Nest agreed, removing the sword from his hands.

Cuscraid smiled. For a brief moment, Nest sensed his thoughts, and that he loved women who knew their own minds. She saw how she reminded him of his lover, Crierwy, and how much it delighted him to see this in a younger person.

"Remember, we have all learned transparency," she reminded him, though she carefully considered his innuendo. She looked down and studied the sword for a few seconds. Instead of putting it away, she decided to place it on the small table near her left.

Cuscraid heavily watched her without further comment. He could see that she was weighing his thoughts. Suddenly, Nest gasped and dropped her head. Running her hand over her head as if to erase a memory, she retrieved a solution from the depths of her consciousness. She looked up at Cuscraid in disbelief and amazement.

"Here, give this stone to Crierwy when you see her again," Nest said, yielding the stone from her pocket. Tears began to fall from her eyes. Wiping them away with her fingers still wrapped around the stone, she quickly handed it to Cuscraid before she changed her mind. It was the Transparency Diamond that Patrick had given Queen Joslin hundreds of years ago.

"That is a very heavy rock to be carrying on your person," Cuscraid said. "It is as big as Alfie's fist."

His dark eyes sized her up. She could feel the gravity of his stare.

Slightly blushing uncomfortably, Nest dried a few more tears from her eyes. Then, she confidently confronted his stare. "Tinka gave it my father. He gave it to me when the twins were born," she responded. "He told me that soul love is transparent. This stone conducts signals of a higher vibrational frequency that can never be heard by the Serpentines or Grays. The communication is invisible, because they are too dense to hear it. At first, only new Dragons like Smoke could hear those frequencies. Now we all can hear these frequencies. That is how far we have come. It is how we can escape detection from the latest Serpentine activities and the eye in the sky. As long as we communicate without coloring the message of love, then we can't be found. Take it to Creirwy. Give her my love."

"Now I understand your tears," he said, turning his head away and pocketing the clear diamond. "Yes, I will bring your finely tuned love with me. You will be seeing this transparent stone again. I know it. It has a way of showing up during the most critical moments of the planet's destiny. It is not destined for the Celestial realm. That I know, too."

Cuscraid rose and Nest understood that it was time to go. Nest threw herself at him in a loving embrace. Together they held each other in front of the fire.

"You must go," he told her. "Hurry before the Serpentines arrive. I must put this place in another dimension. Crierwy will be coming soon. I don't want you to witness these events. It would be too overwhelming for your sensitivities."

"I know," she whispered, releasing him to dry more tears. She backed away. Nest's body shook as her trembling hand reached for her travel bag. She quietly left the cottage without a further word.

"Go get them, tiger," he said softly after the young woman closed the door behind her. Pausing a few moments to reflect on the silence between them, he realized that he had been heard. He smiled to himself and prepared for his final departure.

****

After stepping outside of the cottage, Nest wandered a few yards down the dirt road. She suddenly realized that Cuscraid had called her *tiger* in her absence. As she wondered what he meant by it, a mist rose from across the sea and Nest entered it. Somewhere inside the whiteness of the vapor swirling around her she found Elissa waiting for her. Her golden dragon scales glistened in the watery air as she stood silently to Nest's side.

"There you are," Elissa greeted.

"Why are you here?" she suspiciously asked the golden Sea Dragon queen. "You are supposed to be watching my first born."

"You need me more than he does," Elissa quipped. "He fired me and adopted one of the amber-colored Sea Dragons as his own."

"They grow up so quickly, don't they?" she said almost flippantly. She headed further into the clouds down the road, proudly trying to ignore the Sea Dragon queen. "Get lost."

"C'mon, tiger, let's go make wonderful mischief on Aquitaine together," she proposed.

"Tiger!" Nest stopped to shout. "Have you been talking to Cuscraid?"

"Some truths arise more audibly, if left unspoken," Elissa answered. "Take them out while they sleep."

"I give up. You win. You get to stay," Nest surrendered. "Taking out lions while they sleep is a radical idea. I want to hear more about it. First, let's get out of here, fast."

"Where to?" Elissa politely quizzed her.

"Scotland," she answered firmly. "I want to meet up with Gilderoy's rebellion and the black Fairies."

"What about your first born?" she asked as Nest climbed on her golden scales.

"He has seventeen buddies to look after him. That's sixteen more than me," she replied.

"I'm so glad you love me," Elissa said earnestly. "It took awhile, but it will make things easier."

"No kissing, please," Nest muttered. Immediately changing the subject, the young mother continued, "Let's check and see how Rhodri did in Scotland. I'm still his mom. I only extended his invisible umbilical cord."

"What about the twins?" Elissa asked her.

"Elise is busy training them in jousting etiquette," Nest said. "They can sure use it. Like Cain and Abel, they need to learn how to keep their claws in."

"They will make fierce fighters," Elissa observed.

"If they survive each other." Nest chuckled softly.

Chapter Nineteen

Rather than meet Gilderoy in his mountain cave, Nest flew Elissa to the Callanish landing pad on one of the Hebrides Islands. She intended to meet with the latest group that Gilderoy had enlisted for his Scottish revolution. Several black Fairies emerged from cavities in the stones and greeted her. Nest pulled her travel bag over her shoulder and dismounted. A dark-skinned man emerged from behind one of the standing rocks.

"My name is McPhee," he introduced himself. "How are you doing, Queen Nest? The black Fairies told us that you were coming."

"Glad to have your acquaintance, McPhee," Nest replied. "I understand that your tribe was made up of Dragon flyers on the Congo."

"Yes, we still operate the Congo base, though we have moved our headquarters here on Callanish," McPhee told her. "We've come to join the Scottish rebellion. It serves as a decoy from the Serpentines in Africa. We were inspired by Gilderoy."

"How did you hear about it?" she asked.

"Gilderoy told one of our black Fairies, who passed along the information to the queen," he answered. "The queen of the black Fairies, Mael Maeve, alerted us."

"Is Mael Maeve here too?" Nest questioned, looking around the standing stones for a glittery black Fairy queen. The powerful queen greatly influenced the success of the Soul Transport Network. Nest wanted to make sure the system was still intact, despite the latest Serpentine agenda.

"She waits for us in the forest," McPhee answered. "The Serpentines have been pursuing her lately and she uses the underbrush for cover."

They left the circle of standing stones and walked into the thick forest. Elissa followed close behind, feasting freely on wild edibles while making sure to avoid eating a flighty fairy. After they had fully entered the forest where lush vegetation cloaked them from view in all four directions, the queen of the black Fairies appeared.

"Hello there," a throaty female voice welcomed her.

Nest turned around to see where the voice originated. She spied a tiny dark-skinned Fairy with jet-black wings. The voice seemed three times the size of the fairy.

"I'm glad you came," Mael Maeve continued. "We have been in much danger lately and could use a few solutions."

"We must unite your base with Rhodri's mandala," Nest answered. "It is being gridded with the Transparency Diamond, which Cuscraid is carrying to the other side soon."

"It is the evolution of the Soul Transport System," Mael Maeve remarked, twinkling her shiny ebony wings in random rays of sunlight. "What do you want us to do?"

"Help transport the souls for us. You possess the ability to see between the layers and traverse the many dimensions of life," Nest replied. "You know which souls swim and which ones drown in the Sea of Consciousness."

Mael Maeve smiled. "Yes, the black Fairies swim in the Sea Consciousness like fleeting shadows. We'd be more than happy to cut out the dead weight."

"Thanks," Nest said graciously. Then she turned to McPhee. "We need your band of Dragon flyers to serve as intermediaries."

"We can handle that easily." He grinned at Mael Maeve. "We already are in close communication with the black Fairies."

"Great," Nest responded. "Have you seen any of Rhodri's Sea Dragons? They have a thick, red diamond coat."

"I think we saw her over there in the clearing," McPhee answered. "She was blinding everyone in the sunlight while munching on the wild grass."

"Yes, that's Frieda," Nest commented. "Take good care of her. Rhodri will be back to begin training the next generation of Dragon flyers. This crop of Sea Dragons has much more protection in the Soul Transport System. The shells of the eggs were solid diamonds—the hardest rock there is."

McPhee heaved a whistle with a large sigh. Then he told them, "That brings us hope. No more sabotage during life transitions."

"Elissa, let's go visit Gilderoy and his Scottish rebels," Nest decided as she turned around and headed out of the forest with a light wave to Mael Maeve.

McPhee shook himself gently to recover from the impact of his latest revelation. He told Mael Maeve, "This new queen moves fast. We had better keep up with her."

Mael Maeve nodded in agreement with a light sparkle. She replied in her deep, slow voice. "This woman has three small ones to keep after. She must keep on her toes. Go, follow her."

McPhee turned and ran out of the forest behind Nest. He caught her before she boarded Elissa. He pulled a small pouch from his pocket and handed it to her.

"Here. It's black fairy dust," he mentioned. "Use it in emergencies. It will make you psychologically invisible."

"Thank you," Nest answered as she hurriedly stuffed the pouch in the confines of her cloak.

Nest focused her attention on takeoff as Elissa spread her great golden wings. McPhee stood back from the action. He watched the magnificent sight of a Dragon flyer soar on a golden dragon in the skies above. Then he placed the Callanish landing pad in another dimension with some leftover black fairy dust. Nest watched Callanish disappear from the heights overhead.

When Nest was sure that she would not be overheard, the young mother leaned forward and whispered in Elissa's ear, "What does psychologically invisible mean?"

Chapter Twenty

"I want to be psychologically invisible to my enemies. All this coming and going is annoying," Nest announced when she landed at Gilderoy's outpost. "We are hooked to our spiritual predators. "

"Tell me about it," Gilderoy agreed as he assumed a reclined position in his nest. He placed his feet on a nearby rock. Crossing his hands behind his head, he thought a moment. "What next, boss?"

"No, I changed my mind. I want to do something more assertive than make myself psychologically invisible. It is time to quit hiding. We need to come up with something better than black fairy dust," Nest decided as she folded her arms across her chest and paced the floor of the cave. "Maybe if we quit feeling sorry for our enemies, then we'd be able to get them out of our heads."

"Keep going," Gilderoy said. "I think that you have raised a very important concern."

Elissa watched quietly the interplay between the rebel Sea Dragon and the young mother. She was amazed at how Gilderoy handled the feisty, young queen in a concerned deft manner. Gilderoy's communication skills had gone unnoticed until now. Instinctively, Nest sought his counsel. The larger his rebellion grew, the more Gilderoy mellowed.

"What is it that keeps us tied to them?" Nest questioned. "It is painful."

"These are deep questions," Gilderoy reflected. "I don't know why we didn't dump them in the Celestial realm."

"Now we have to deal with the infiltrated human side as well," Nest continued. "They pretend to care, we reattach, and then they abandon us. Abandonment is a serious crime in the spiritual dimensions."

"Keep going," Gilderoy repeated.

"We must be building our immunity or something," she reflected. "Eventually we'll get to the end of all this futility."

"Immunity," Gilderoy echoed.

"There must be more than that," Nest continued.

"There is," Gilderoy said thoughtfully. "Carry on."

"It must be part of the exchange program," Nest said. "They kept Pellinor in order to learn more about wrinkling time."

"True," Gilderoy encouraged. "That was painful."

"Enough of this. No more exchange programs," Nest proposed. "We must seize the initiative rather than wait for them to decide whether they are friend or foe. I need more breathing space."

"What a revolutionary concept!" Gilderoy marveled, putting his feet down and rising from his bed.

"They act as if I was born yesterday," Nest said as she looked at Gilderoy in the eye.

"Well, yes," he told her. "Compared to the age of the others, you were."

"Well, maybe you are right," Nest realized as she stopped in her tracks.

"It is not your fault," he said. "Your children are training you."

Nest bowed her head with an air of defeat, "Now what?"

"It's a problem with Original Innocence," Gilderoy observed putting his hands on Nest's arms to steady her. "It led to Original Wound , rather than Original Sin."

Nest sighed. She reluctantly looked into Gilderoy's eyes and pleaded, "What next?"

"Whatever you lack in skill and wisdom, you make up for with hormones and passion," Gilderoy told her. "You come loaded with it. Being good with a sword is an additional asset. I heard about how you removed Lucky's implant from a vital area. He trusted you with his heart."

"Thanks," Nest said. "So far it seems to be working."

"I know," he said, tossing his head slightly.

Nest turned her head slightly away from his stare. "Let's go to Scarborough Fair."

"Why?" Gilderoy asked tightening his grip on the young queen so that she was forced to face him.

"The descendants of Nimue live in Yorkshire and have maintained a foothold in Northumbria," Nest said as she wiggled out of Gilderoy's grip. "They escape detection. Nobody bothers them."

"Keep going," he replied, releasing her. "I'll come along with you and Elissa."

******

The next morning, two Sea Dragons and Nest arrived at the Scarborough Fair in York. They wandered the fairgrounds until they found a vendor with parsley, sage, rosemary, and thyme. No one saw the Sea Dragons. Nest had thrown black fairy dust on them.

"Smells good," Gilderoy commented.

Elissa strayed over to the vendor with the henna body paint.

"Stay here," Nest commanded the Sea Dragon queen in a hushed voice.

"Did you say something?" the young monk selling the herbs asked. Something about the vendor seemed familiar. "I know your Sea Dragons," he told her in a low voice.

"Why, Kuan Yin? What ever made you decide to incarnate?" Nest confronted the vendor, who happened to be a young monk.

"Earl," he replied. "I fell for a young priest at the abbey. We exchanged vows."

"I see that you took it literally," Nest remarked. "The change is hopeful. I am glad to see that you are healing. You must be giving men another try after your tryst with Buddha."

"Yes, I am very happy with Earl," the monk agreed.

In celebration, the Sea Dragons danced for joy. Nest threw more black fairy dust on them to keep their jubilance from being noticed. She noticed that whatever the people did not see psychologically, they did not see at all. Nest made a note of this cultural phenomenon.

"Can you tell me where I can find the descendants of Nimue?" Nest asked the monk with the herbs.

"Oh, the Sawdons," he began. "They became followers of Bridget, the Green Knight crucified by the Serpentines. They were not related by blood. They sort of made a cult out of it."

"Sounds interesting," Nest said. Getting down to business, she asked the young monk directly, "Where are they?"

"Just outside of town. The King of Yorkshire is a Sawdon."

"Great," Nest said. Then she turned to the Sea Dragons, who were doing the polka in the streets. "C'mon guys, we are going to have a queen-to-king discussion in Yorkshire."

"Wonderful!" Elissa exclaimed, who had started dancing on the tables.

"Thank you, Kuan Yin.... or, what is your new name?" Nest asked.

"Kilroy," the monk said. "Here. Take some rosemary. It is for remembrance."

"Thanks." Nest said as she reached across the table to hug the monk.

"Oh, oh," the monk said. "No hugs. The Serpentines are still in charge of Northumbria. They define celibacy by the abstinence of opposite sex relationships."

"Now, are we really that opposite?" Nest asked. She loved the spirit inside the monk.

"No, of course not, but they don't know that," the handsome monk answered. "We are one big happy family."

"You know, you're kind of cute as a male," Nest mischievously told him.

"Stop it," the monk insisted. "Here, have some sage too!"

"Glad to see you're back and playing again," Nest said as she backed away. "See you later. I have a Sawdon to talk to."

****

Moments later, Nest was knocking on the heavy wooden door of the king's castle.

"What's the password?" the guard at the door asked.

"Nobody's business," Nest recalled.

"OK, come in," the guard said. "The Sea Dragons can go forage in the woods in back." The guard led her down a hall to a room with a blazing fire.

A man reclined in a large soft chair offered a seat to Nest. "Sit down," he told her.

"I'll make it brief," Nest began. "I have to get back to my twins and son. My husband is probably pulling his hair out by now."

"Been there. Done that," the King of Yorkshire said.

"Great," said Nest. " We understand each other. Tell me, why are you guys followers of Bridget?"

"Nothing better to do," he told her truthfully.

"Now, listen," Nest said. "Don't jerk with me. Why? This lovely Green Knight died a horrible death."

"That is not what we see," the King of Yorkshire confessed. "We see the life and the earth spirits that she represented. What a celebration!"

"You're right," Nest admitted. "That's all I need to know. I love you. See you later. Keep in touch."

The King of Yorkshire looked at her and sighed. Without ever bothering to rise from his chair, he watched Nest leave the room and head for the door. Instead he waved his hand lightly as if to say, *Carry on.*

Chapter Twenty-One

"Those girls ran me ragged," Elise confessed when Nest returned. "They are so competitive. I don't know how you managed to deliver them with a toddler underfoot. How come you haven't lost your mind yet?"

"What makes you think that I haven't?" Nest questioned rhetorically. "I've been wrestling with Gilderoy over futility issues." Then she chuckled. "Only joking. We haven't lost it yet. Can we just lock the door and throw away the key?"

"You've got your man," he admitted as he rose from his chair by the fire. He approached Nest with open arms. "I can see that you've had a long trip."

"It was a trip," Nest agreed. "I need you."

"I know," he said as he carefully removed her clothes. "We have twenty minutes before one of the twins wakes."

"No problem," she said, falling into his arms.

Elise succinctly removed every thread from her body. When he was satisfied with his work, he carried his nude wife to the floor.

"It is time to ground this flight," he demanded as he thrust himself inside her.

"Carry on," she sighed deeply. "I delegate my authority. You know me."

"Very well," he said with confidence as he entered her a second time.

Nest soared. "You'll never get me down," she said.

"I know," he told her as he kissed her ear.

The couple lapsed into a peaceful silence. Ten minutes later, the twins burst into the room. Finding their parents naked on the floor in a glued embrace, they rolled their eyes at each other with irritated sighs.

"They're at it again," Esyllt, the light-haired child complained to the dark-haired one.

"Let's get out of here," Angharad, the dark-haired twin added. "I'll show you my secret hiding fort in the meadows. One of Rhodri's Dragons has been helping me build it."

Both girls shrugged simultaneously, then turned and faced each other. Angharad took the hand of her sister and together they hurried out of the room. Esyllt tossed her head at her parents as they ran out of sight.

"I thought you locked the door," Nest whispered in Elise's ear.

"I suppose that it won't be the first ball that gets dropped today," he admitted. Then he changed the subject and raised his head from her breast. "Maybe we inadvertently taught the twins a lesson in cooperation. Great to have you back, dear."

"They missed the action. Nothing was exposed except their father's hips," Nest said as she tapped his buttocks lightly with a hint of ownership.

"So much for exposure. I was only reflecting the moon." he replied. "Though, I am perplexed by their lack of shock."

"Obviously, they are getting bored with us," Nest said, sitting up to kiss Elise's cheek. "It is just all hormones and passion."

"What next?" he asked.

"Let's double lock and barricade the door," Nest suggested. "Then we can catch up on our sleep while the twins play."

Two hours later, the couple emerged from closed doors, refreshed. They checked on the twins and found them contentedly playing in the meadow with several amber-colored diamond Sea Dragons. Intent on their activity, the two girls smiled briefly at their parents and ignored them.

"How about a short walk?" Elise proposed as he directed Nest toward the woods.

"Great idea," Nest agreed. "We can watch the children as I discuss things with the black Fairies."

"Are the black Fairies helping now?" Elise asked.

"Yes, the African Fairies are assisting with the Soul Transport System," Nest said. "It is the latest innovation."

Stepping few yards inside the wooden area, they found a black Fairy perched on top of a large fern. The couple could see the children playing in the distance. Turning toward the black Fairy, they watched the sunlight illumine the dew crystals on his dark wings. His body glistened like a black diamond.

"I've been waiting for you," the black Fairy told them. "I brought you something from behind the veil. Look under the fern."

Nest and Elise did as he advised them. Together they began gently turning over the leaves of the lush green fern. At the base of the plant, concealed between several leaves, Elise spied a glimmering object. Rather than pick it up, he called his lover over to his side.

"Here it is," he said, ushering Nest over to the object in front of him.

"It's the Transparency Diamond!" she cried, clasping her hands over her heart in joy. She kissed Elise and picked up the stone. "My father gave it to me when the twins were born."

"How did you get it here?" Elise asked the black Fairy.

"McPhee found it at the Callanish stone circle. He took it to Mael Maeve and she confirmed the identity of the Transparency Diamond. McPhee borrowed Rhodri's Sea Dragon and gave it me. Cuscraid succeeded in carrying the Transparency Diamond across the veil. Wishing to close the circle, I gave it to him on impulse as a way of extending my love to my predecessor, Crierwy. Nicholas and I are doing her job now, and I wanted her blessing. Here it is. Cuscraid said that the stone has a way of showing up at the most critical moments in history."

"Why didn't McPhee stop by the suite?" Elise asked, changing the subject at a pivotal moment. Unlike Nicholas, he contended that his job was to help Nest focus on more earth-bound issues, such as the Kingdom of the Golden Tara.

"You two were busy," the black Fairy said with a deep, sexy voice and a grin.

"Oh." Nest gave a light shrug. "At least McPhee didn't come barging in like the twins."

"Mael Maeve suggests that you grid the Transparency Diamond in the Four Directions. Use the system at the Hill of Tara," the black Fairy mentioned. "Insert the Transparency Diamond opposite the Fairy Tree in the east."

"Wonderful! This will tie the Kingdom of the Golden Tara with loved ones behind the veil, which keeps us out of the reach of the Serpentines and Grays. I have managed my distance with these enemies for many years," Nest responded. "We'll take the girls. It is time they start learning Dragon flying and planetary gridding, while Rhodri sets up base camp in Scotland. I just finished checking up on him. He needs to prepare before accepting trainees, especially these two girls."

"Thank you very much," Elise told the black Fairy. "We will get on it right away." The couple headed for the meadow and called the girls.

"Start packing for your first Dragon flight!" Nest yelled to them at the edge of the woods.

The twins dropped their game immediately and ran toward the abbey suite. "We get to fly a dragon!" they told each other in unison.

Holding hands, they raced across the field and rushed to their room. Nest found them hurling clothes in the air as they competed for the fastest packer. Several amber-colored diamond Sea Dragons entered the room behind Nest.

"I'll let you women figure out what to wear while I tell Elissa and the others," Elise said.

****

Moments later, the family converged in the woods outside the abbey along with Elissa and Curtis. Each parent took a child aboard their Sea Dragons and strapped them to the dragon's body. The Sea Dragons spread their great wings and soared high in the sky. Delighted, the girls could barely contain their emotions.

Landing on the western site of the Four Directions grid, they quickly dismounted. The parents helped the children put their feet on the ground. Immediately, they began exploring the terrain. Nest and Elise remained a few steps behind as the twins peered underneath every fallen log and embedded stone.

"Welcome to the Hill of Tara," a black Fairy greeted from a black elderberry.

Several black Fairies fluttered overhead, lighting the dense brush with beautiful streaks of dark violet light.

"Mom, it's beautiful," Angharad, the dark-haired twin commented, looking up at the tree.

"See, Dad? It's a pretty raven feather," Esyllt, the light-haired twin said, examining the ground underneath the tree. "There're two of them."

"Use the raven feather to summon the black Fairies," the black Fairy instructed. "The raven feather represents transitions. They are not always peaceful."

"Here girls, take this Transparency Diamond and put it in the hollow of the elderberry," Nest instructed. "You each may have a raven feather."

"We are freeing ourselves from the chains that have been around human and Celestial existence, and invoking the wisdom of the Fairies. Your mother and Lucky moved the traumatized human spirit from the Tree of Knowledge to the Boab Tree of Freedom. With the connection to this particular Fairy tree, we are adding a little magic of love and light, inspired by the earth spirits," Elise told them.

"Creirwy's mission was undertaken by Nest with the help of two men, your father and Nicholas," the black Fairy remarked. "The collective work of these three people creates a special kind of energy that Patrick knew as a trinity. Patrick was the one who gave the Transparency Diamond to King Arthur's sister, Joslin, when all hope seemed lost hundreds of years ago."

One child palmed the Transparency Diamond, while the other brushed her raven feather. Both reflected on the words of their father, and remained awed by the process. Elise waited for the girls to collect their thoughts, before continuing.

"Never again will the Soul Transport System be as vulnerable as it was in ancient Egypt. A lot of Serpentines disguised as crocodiles took out the souls crossing the Nile River. They assumed the form of a reptile with a big mouth to swim in the waters of spirit and consciousness. He was a consumer and spiritual predator. Putting the Transparency Diamond in this particular Fairy tree makes the migrating souls invisible to dark forces in the universe. Both of you will help your brother protect his kingdom, which is an extension of the ones that your mother and I operate. The Serpentine Romans only make paper trails, whereas ours are extensive grids of light and love. It is important to have crosschecks in case something gets lost or forgotten. Nobody is perfect, but we all do are best given the circumstances."

Peacefully, the girls tucked the stone in the recess of the tree. Then they held each other's hand and gazed contentedly at the glowing diamond that now studded the tree's trunk. The black Fairies surrounded the diamond, basking in its refracted light.

21283553R00064

Made in the USA
Charleston, SC
12 August 2013